Dear Sarah —
I'm so proud of you and grateful to know you!
Here's to suc[cess]
T. H

Certainty

WALKING THROUGH FIRE

Know you are loved and Families are Forever!

Tanya Harris Rounds

Certainty
WALKING THROUGH FIRE

TANYA HARRIS ROUNDY

DRMAJNKE UNLIMITED

For information contact:
drmajnke2020@gmail.com
Website: sites.google.com/view/tanya-harris-roundy-author

Published by:
Drmajnke Unlimited

Copy Editor: Kim Autrey • Content Editor: Debbie Ihler Rasmussen
Cover design by Santo Roy • SantoRoy71
Interior book design by Francine Platt, Eden Graphics, Inc.

Paperback ISBN   978-1-958626-58-0
eBook ISBN   978-1-958626-59-7
Audio ISBN   978-1-958626-60-3

Library of Congress Number: 2023918060

Manufactured in the United States of America

First Edition

To my loving patient husband and children.

For my family, on both sides of the veil.

PROLOGUE

ERTAINTY wasn't a word in their vocabulary. Time on the clock slowed to forever.

The once family of seven was now only five. The loss was unbearable.

Glowing embers burned in their minds, along with the faces of their lost little ones.

Why? Just why?

Certainty… Certainty could never be a word in their vocabulary.

Yet, the clock's hands still moved forward; time moved forward without them.

Through it all, light found its way in.

CHAPTER ONE

MARIA MARKSWORTH woke early Christmas morning. Pine scent spilled through the cracked door, awakening her sleepy senses as hazy darkness serenely enveloped the room. She listened intently to the soft breathing at her side.

No little giggles or sneaking footsteps… yet.

She gently rolled over to face her husband. She held the blankets close to her chest, so they didn't move too much. Her eyes adjusted in the darkness as she gazed at him.

Laugh lines permanently creased the corners of his crystal blue eyes. She lifted her finger and softly traced his strong, straight jawline. Dimples imprinted the edges of his mouth; his soft skin lightly browned from working in the sun.

What could not be seen, but what she knew, was the goodness of this man's heart, the patience and love for her and their family.

She couldn't remember a time without him by her side, without his sturdy strength.

Memories raced back to college English class. A teacher droned onto a question, likely meant to be rhetorical when suddenly a deep voice pierced the monotony.

Slightly sarcastic, his comment was poignant and took the teacher off guard. It made Maria smile.

Who is he?

She had wondered and made it a mental note to continue discussing that comment. Later that afternoon, a shadow crossed her path while she studied in the quad. She looked up. It was the same guy who had commented in class earlier. She didn't want to let the chance slip by, so she shouted, "Hey, that was a cool comment on postmodernism."

Shocked at her boldness, she bit her lip and worried he wouldn't appreciate being called out like that.

But he stopped, turned his head, and smiled. She felt her face blush; flutters rushed through her stomach. At that moment, she somehow knew there was something, and that they would always be together.

Sharing the same English class led to incredible conversations. They had debates about life, politics, and even topics that might seem mundane to some.

They didn't agree on everything, but their differences made for healthy and enlightening discussions, strengthening their respect for each other. Once they started into matters of philosophy and religions, the conversations got pretty heated. For a while, Maria was unsure they could get over their different views on religion.

While she believed that there might be a church or religion that could fit her feelings, Steve believed in the idea of a Supreme Being, but he did not think that any church could tell one what they should or should not believe.

In the end, even in matters of faith that were important to her, they had found common ground and a way to understand and appreciate each other's values.

This issue, however, plagued her life. When she was a teenager, her parents criticized her for her lack of faith, but her decision to marry Steve outside of their church upset them more than she could have imagined.

Her parents barely spoke at their wedding and only visited briefly before Steve and Maria gave them grandchildren.

This arrangement suited Maria. She didn't want to argue anymore on the subject. But there were times when she questioned her choices, especially at Christmas. She missed her family and what it might have been like to have them there.

But she and Steve had come together and found a way that worked, and that's what she valued in him and their relationship. She truly felt that is what God would want most, peace and love in a family doing their best.

They were married just short of ten years now. People had laughed at and mocked them for only dating three months before becoming engaged and were even more appalled that they only had two months before the wedding.

Deep in their hearts, they knew it was right, so why wait? Nothing else but each other seemed to matter, and she did not regret that choice. But now, could it be ten years? It had passed so quickly, and yet so much had happened. There had been hard times, more than she wanted to admit. A year after they were married, she became pregnant and quit school. She felt strongly about being at home with her children. She never regretted her choice, despite the voices around her, even those from her family. They told her to get her career in place first, but to Maria, her family was her career. They were her life.

Over the years, she had taken courses one by one and finished her degree at night, but she did not want to leave her home to go to school or work. That proved to be challenging at times. Their family had quickly grown and lived on Steve's teacher salary. But now, as she looked at him, all the hardships had been worth it to have him here beside her and their children.

She knew Steve often worried that he didn't provide enough for them. Yes, they had their struggles, but they never wanted the necessities, and there was always an abundance of joy and laughter in their house, making her love him even more.

A sudden ache came over her as she touched his cheek, and the pang concerned her. She listened and waited, but nothing. The phone didn't ring, and she buried the feeling, at least for now.

Steve rolled onto his side, put his arm around her, and pulled her close. She closed her eyes and fell asleep, secure in the comfort that he was there.

CHAPTER TWO

STEVE WOKE to the faint footsteps of their oldest child, Jeffrey, was hurrying past their open bedroom door.

A smile crossed his lips, and he pulled Maria closer. He loved the smell of her hair; it reminded him of the essence of peach on the summer wind, and he nestled his head into her neck.

He rested his head on hers and thought about the first time he had seen her. Even then, she had reminded him of summer with her long golden curls, blue eyes, and soft white skin. Her voice sounded like a bird in the breeze.

He was never the same again. How had he ever lived without Maria?

Steve's dad died when Steve was a teenager, and after that, Steve felt he had been slowly dying. Losing his dad had been an enormous hardship for their family, and Steve had given up on true happiness.

But then, there was Maria, breathing life back into his soul. It was as if laughter and love never truly existed until he met her. She was the epitome of goodness and brought out the good in him.

Her contagious smile kept him going even through the births and raising their five children. Steve was a teacher, and she was often alone with the kids while he worked multiple jobs to make ends meet.

He remembered their wedding day, her beautiful simple gown, a crown of flowers in her hair, and a single rose in her hands. At that moment, he thanked whatever higher powers there were. She had smiled and blushed when they spoke their vows, "to love and to cherish until death do us part."

With that thought, a chill instantly ran down his spine and darkened his spirits, but he shook it off and snuggled his face deeper into Maria's hair and neck.

Her family was her life. Nothing else mattered.

He whispered in her ear, "Maria. It's Christmas!"

Especially at this time of year, she reminded him of all he had ever imagined Christmas to be, and somehow, she managed to keep that feeling around him all year.

Her eyes still shut; Maria smiled. They lingered in each other's arms, and he marveled at how rich their life had become.

A squeal from the living room brought them both out of bed.

"Santa came!"

They pulled their robes on and tried to contain their excitement as they hurried to the living room, greeted by beaming smiles and the glow of the lights. All but their youngest gathered around the tree, and it was hard to tell which was brighter, the tree or the smiles on their children's faces.

Oh, to be young again!

If the kids only knew about the late hours and the hard work it had taken to put together this meager Christmas for them. There wasn't much, a few gifts for each child and some fruit and chocolate in their stockings. But to them, it was as if they were entering an amusement park.

Maria went to get their youngest, Sarah, while Steve helped the kids with their stockings. He let them dive in while he captured pictures of each treasure and smiled.

CHAPTER THREE

*TEVE SAT QUIETLY in his overstuffed chair and watched the
magic in their excited children's eyes.

The spitting image of his father, eight-year-old Jeffrey, was
bright-eyed, strong-spirited, darkly handsome, and a strong
leader for his siblings. His excitement fueled the others.

Maria always said she could see great things coming from
him. In school, he was well ahead of his classmates and enjoyed
the attention, but it led to a lot of teasing and bullying from
other kids his age.

Despite this, he had a few good friends and was always kind,
loving, and generous. Sometimes it seemed he was too giving,
but how could you find fault with such innocence and love?

Jeffrey's eyes lit up when he opened a package of new books.
They chose a few of his favorites from the used section of the
library and a couple of new ones.

His eyes widened. "Wow, thanks, Mom! Tommy and Braxton are gonna love these!"

Maria knew Jeffrey would loan the books, but it was okay
because Tommy and Braxton were his best friends.

With soft auburn curls to her shoulders and an angled face, seven-year-old Lori was small and shy. Her dark blue eyes often gave the impression she was sad. Yet, she seemed to know others' feelings and could make them smile if needed.

Steve thought of the day of her birth when she almost didn't make it. She was too early, and he feared the worst. He and Maria had spent countless hours sitting by her isolette, worrying that she might never come home with them. Their home was never the same when she finally did.

She brought a calming influence, a sensitive spirit, and the knack for knowing when he needed a hug. He wanted to protect her from the world because he knew she could easily be hurt. But right now, the new little doll with homemade dresses brought a sparkle into her eyes, and that made him smile.

He laughed, watching five-year-old Allan and Patrick, their little troublemaker twins. Both arrived early, healthy, and full of energy that had never stopped. Different as night and day in looks, Allan, a toe-headed blond with pleasing pale blue eyes, and Patrick, stick straight, mud brown hair whose hazel eyes sparkled with life.

However different in looks, their personalities were two halves coming together in each antic. They seemed to know what the other was thinking and communicated in their own language.

Maria often said she knew they were in trouble somewhere if she couldn't hear them. They loved to sneak up on her while she was cooking and ambush her from either side. Patrick and Allan filled their home with excitement and entertainment.

Steve marveled at their imagination as they turned their new homemade blocks and used Lincoln logs into a fort and battle weapons.

Maria came into the room with their youngest, three-year-old Sarah, and he stood and joined the two of them on the sofa. He could see that Sarah wasn't sure what was happening, but her eyes intently followed her brothers and sister.

Small for her age with dusty blond hair that shaped her round face, her wide brown eyes expressed what she couldn't say. Sarah was born with spina bifida, meaning her spine was outside her body. They knew she would have limitations; however, difficulties multiplied along the way, eventually rendering her physical and mental development a year or two behind those her age.

At first, Maria struggled mentally and emotionally with how to care for her and still keep up with the other children. She was overwhelmed with the machines used to help her breathe, doctor appointments, and how to manage her time.

Steve's mother Lois had been a Godsend, and soon Maria learned to manage with Lois' help. After the first couple months, her heart had given way to the unspeakable love of a mother for her child, and Sarah became Maria's solace and joy.

On the other hand, Steve had latched onto her from the first moment, wrapping her strings around his heart. Sarah was the light in the family's life, and her siblings adored her and would often carry her everywhere she wanted to go and then some.

Steve and Maria watched from a distance when Jeffrey read books to Sarah, explaining the pictures as she cooed and looked on wide-eyed. Sometimes they would catch Lori snuggling with her in her crib.

Sarah giggled when the twins entertained her, and the three of them never seemed to tire of the fun; it could go on for hours.

Deciding what to get Sarah for Christmas this year had been hard. Her hands could not open anything without help, and she couldn't walk.

So, they found a wagon and fixed it up. Maria made a new blanket and a couple of matching pillows, and when they set Sarah in it, the others began pulling her around, and her eyes lit up. Maria's filled with tears.

Steve took in the scene before him, and his heart swelled joyfully. He turned to Maria and took her hand. How had they been so blessed? At this moment, his life felt complete.

Again, a menacing chill down his spine, and darkness overshadowed this happy moment. He closed his eyes, blackness. He opened them and noticed Maria's concerned look.

He smiled, squeezed her hand, and stood. "Okay, who wants pancakes?"

Squeals of joy and jumping kids followed him into the kitchen.

Maria followed them, but she was in no hurry to leave the tranquil moment. She secretly wished things would never change, but life is temporary; she knew that.

Her beautiful family was temporary, too, but she committed to relishing each precious moment.

If only they could stay little a little longer.

CHAPTER FOUR

STEVE WAS Lois Marksworth's youngest child. With three boys and no daughters, she had aged more quickly than she liked. Short, plump around the middle, with a head of white hair and spectacles over her gray eyes, she wanted to think of herself as Mrs. Santa Claus.

The kids loved their Grandma Marksworth and her beautiful stories full of fantasy and adventure. With Sarah on her lap, she often gathered the others around her on the old green flowered couch. She entertained them for hours with tales of knights, kings, princesses, and witches. Maria could see their grandma seemed to love telling them how she could see their future, and she spent every minute with Steve and his family.

Steve waited for his mom to answer the phone.

"Hi, Mom."

"Merry Christmas, Steve. How was your day?"

"Great! It was so fun to watch the children this morning. We have lots of pictures for you, too. Are you coming over later?"

"Yes, after I talk to your brothers, you can expect me for dinner, okay? Hug the kids and tell them Granny is on the way."

"All right, Mom, love you. See you in a bit."

Steve hung up the phone. He was always in awe at his mother's strength, especially after his dad died. At the time, his two older brothers were away at college, and he was still in high school. His mother had never received her formal education or worked outside the home, so life had become difficult for a long time.

Steve could have been more helpful. Hurt, angry, and unsure of his feelings, let alone how to express them, he took anger out on his mom and himself, especially in the first year. He often heard his mother crying in her room at night, guilt piercing his heart, yet teenage boy angst prevented him from doing what he knew he probably should have.

But that started to change his junior year. Mr. Hinckle, a teacher who didn't allow Steve's hard, angry exterior to deter kindness or the attention Steve so desperately needed. Slowly, he was able to help him use words to express what he was going through. Things improved with his mom, and they found a way to move forward together.

Mr. Hinckle was a significant factor in Steve becoming a teacher himself.

His brothers worked their way into well-paying jobs and began to help their mom and provide her with a comfortable life. But his brothers lived so far away that Steve's family had become her sole contact and joy.

She was a great help to Maria with the children and occasionally gave her much-needed breaks.

Was it possible that he was good enough to have these two wonderful women in his life?

He turned around to see Maria at the kitchen sink. He pulled her to him and kissed her gently, then he smiled.

"What was that for?" she asked.

"For being here, with me, right here and now. I know it's not always been easy."

She snickered.

"And I'm sure it will never be," he added. "But here you are, and I love you."

He kissed her again, and they held each other for a few minutes before being interrupted by the twins.

Patrick yelled, "On guard!" and Maria yelped.

"Touche," yelled Allan. He jabbed the Lincoln log, now turned fencing sword, at his brother.

Steve grabbed them both with a roar, and Maria smiled as they ran away squealing.

Their small, three-bedroom trailer house sat on a foundation but had little room to spare. Soon after Jeffrey was born, Steve got a teaching position at the local high school, allowing them to buy the house.

The cubicle of a kitchen had barely enough room for both of them, but they didn't mind. They usually managed to flow around each other, but the addition of the twin's battle wasn't helping.

Steve said, "I'll be more help if I go get the kids down for a nap before Mom comes."

Maria just smiled. "I'll join you in a minute."

Steve walked into the living room. "Time to clean up."

Moans chorused through the group, except for Sarah, who smiled and reached for Steve to pick her up, and she laid her head on his shoulder.

"All right then, whoever picks up the most toys will get to pick the nap time story."

Jeffrey quickly slipped into action, and the rest followed. There wasn't much to clean up, but for a tiny living room with barely enough room for the couch and tree, it was like a tidal wave had rolled in, leaving the whole coral reef behind.

But, with all of them cleaning up, even Sarah (with a bit of help from Steve), they finished quickly and chose a new book from Jeffrey's presents.

Maria stood in the doorway, once again amazed at her husband. Children seemed to flock to him. Even at school, he was among the most respected and well-liked teachers. Boys with no fathers or who may have a tough family life seemed to gravitate toward him naturally. That was one of the reasons he had chosen teaching, especially high school. He remembered his rough years without a father, and he hoped to help some of them.

He always tried to be there for his students because of this. It sometimes intruded on their family schedule and often upset Maria, but she now understood that it was important for other children to feel just as loved as her own. If she could share a bit of him, that was the least she could do.

Maria listened and watched for a few more minutes, then joined them and pulled Lori onto her lap, who cuddled in and fell asleep. The story ended a few minutes later, and the twins grumbled.

"Why do we need a nap?" complained Allan, and Patrick added, "Yeah, we're grown up now." But they both rubbed their eyes and yawned. Jeffrey had been up early, so he went with the twins. Maria and Steve went to Lori's bedroom and put her in bed. They converted the office to accommodate Sarah's needs.

They got her hooked up and settled, then they, too, took a nap as the smell of fresh bread and ham began to permeate the tiny home.

That evening as they sat around the table, Lois Marksworth thought of how proud she was of who Steve had become and wished that her husband and Steve's father could have lived to see this. She liked to believe that her husband was somewhere, maybe watching over them. She hadn't learned about God or life after death. But inside, there was something that told her there was. She had taught her sons this, yet only one had been interested. Their lives were full of each other, and Sundays were family time spent in the mountains or having dinner with friends, and that was enough.

She always worried about Steve, though, especially when he was younger. He had so many questions and struggles with everything, and he never seemed satisfied. Then, when his father died, his teenage anger turned him away from anything and everything that suggested a higher power, and he turned bitter and distanced himself from the family. She had worried, struggled, cried, and prayed desperately during that time, not just for her loss but for her son to find peace somehow.

Luckily a teacher at the school had taken him under his wing. Steve latched onto Mr. Hinckle, who gave him stability. He became an influential father figure, guiding and helping Steve channel his feelings. Still, Steve always seemed angry and hopeless, especially regarding anything long-term.

She felt a prayer answered when he met Maria. He had gained more stability in the last several years with the birth of each of their children. The light in his eyes had returned, but tonight she saw a sadness she hadn't seen for a very long time, and it concerned her.

"Grandma," Jeffrey mumbled through a mouthful of food, "I have this cool book Santa brought me… do you want to see it?"

She laughed; he was so like his father. "Probably not right this minute, but we could read some of it later together if you'd like."

He beamed, swallowed, and took another bite.

The twins took this as their turn to talk over the top of each other.

Patrick muddled, "We got tinker toys, and we made them into swords…"

Allan jumped in. "And we had an epic battle with Dad in the kitchen."

"So cool!" in near unison.

Maria and Lois exchanged looks and laughed, but Steve beamed with pride.

"And what did you get, Lori?" Lois looked her granddaughter in the eyes.

"A doll," Lori responded timidly with a grin.

"Wow! I bet you'll be a great mommy to that doll. Did you give her a name?"

"Sammy." She glowed from the praise.

The twins then chimed in with excitement again, all about the wagon and how they took Sarah on adventures. They shared their antics, making Lois feel happiness like she had never known before. This is what life was about, to know and love so deeply, and nothing could be greater.

After dinner, the family gathered on the couch. Sarah curled in Lois' lap with Lori on her side. The twins and Jeffrey crowded over each other on the floor while Steve and Maria listened from the kitchen as they put away the last of the dishes.

Lois' voice read in clear, different, distinct voices stories about bears, little girls lost in the woods, princesses found asleep in towers.

As Maria stepped into the doorway, she felt happy. Truly and magnificently happy. If nothing else was certain – this moment, her children and Steve were. Comforted by this thought, she joined Lois on the couch, allowing Sarah to crawl into her lap for some mommy time.

Lois hugged Steve before she got into her car. "I'll see you later tomorrow?"

"Yeah, I know you have a few things to do, but the kids would love to run around with you. I don't know if Maria has anything planned. I'll let you know if anything changes, though."

"Okay. I love you. I'll see you then."

Steve watched the car drive away and wondered at his mother's strength. He had always known she loved him, that he could return home at any time. He had learned, though, at that moment, that home wasn't a place; it was wherever she was with her open arms waiting for him.

The front door cracked open, and the light formed a halo around Maria as she peeked out. "You coming? The kids are ready to say good night."

"Yeah… coming…"

"You okay?" She looked directly into his eyes. "Seems like something is on your mind today?" She closed the door but didn't turn away from him.

He shrugged. "I'm sure it's nothing. Let's get the kids tucked in."

She touched his face with her hand and let it sit as they lingered together.

CHAPTER FIVE

STEVE WALKED INTO a dark field, unsure where to go. A looming haze surrounded him, and he felt oppressed by blackness. He strained his eyes and searched for someone, anyone; an uneasy sickness sat in the pit of his stomach.

A sulfurous stench choked him, and a piercing noise stung his ears. Frantically, he searched around him, but he couldn't see anything.

He gasped; his eyes jerked open, and now he heard it.

"Maria! Maria!" he yelled, "It's the fire alarm!"

Startled awake, Maria jumped out of bed.

When Steve pulled the door open, a rush of black engulfed them.

Choking, Maria screamed, "Kids!!"

She rushed into the hallway and turned into the first bedroom with Steve at her heels.

She grabbed Lori from her bed, still screaming, "Kids! Kids!"

Steve hurried into Jeffrey's room and shook the bottom bunk bed.

Jeffrey's eyes rolled open. Obviously, in a daze, he climbed out of bed and stumbled toward his dad.

Steve panicked when he grabbed at the top bunk, "Patrick!"

Jeffrey yelled at his dad, "Patrick's here with me!"

Steve grabbed Patrick's arm and pulled Jeffrey out the door with him.

Flames crawled across the ceiling, and heat penetrated his lungs with the smell of burned plastic and campfire.

They stumbled through the smoke, following Marie and Lori out the front door.

Panicked, Maria screamed at Steve, "Where's Allan?"

Horror filled his eyes when Steve yelled, "Jeffrey, go call 911! Lori, go with him!"

Steve and Maria hurried back into the house, choking through the smoke. They both found their way to the small nursery room with Sarah and her equipment. Trying to breathe through the thickened air, they were unfazed by the disappearing walls. Maria at last found and grabbed the doorknob but screamed in pain. She forced her other hand to help turn the knob that seemed welded shut. An acrid stench of metal and burning wires seared her throat and scorched her nostrils. She felt the heat burning into her brain.

Finally, the door jerked open; flames engulfed the entire room. Heat licked at Maria's legs and blinded her; she sputtered, still hopelessly screaming, "Sarah! Allan!" She had to get to them.

Holding his arm over his mouth, Steve pushed past her to the crib finding Sarah wrapped in Allan's arms. Neither of them was moving.

He grabbed Sarah and nearly tossed her to Maria, who barely caught her in her arms.

Blinded by the scorching heat and smoke, she stumbled through the interminable distance between her and the door.

Finally, the cool air hit her face, and she nearly fell off the steps. She found Jeffrey across the yard, holding Lori's sobbing frame, and Patrick nearby, rocking back and forth and staring at the flames.

Maria collapsed next to them and looked back at the house. Where was Steve? "Steve!!"

She tried to scream, but her voice was hoarse, and the words disappeared into the roaring flames that now engulfed the house!

"STEVE!" Sarah's weight in her arms caused her to look at her still-sleeping child.

But something was different. Sarah wasn't moving.

"No, no, no!" Maria put her mouth over Sarah's and forced air into her lungs.

Breathe! Please! Just Breathe!

"DAD!" Jeffrey yelled.

Maria saw Steve working his way from the back of the house. With Allan cradled in his arms and covered with soot, they blended into the darkness that emanated around the flames.

Steve laid Allan on the ground and began CPR.

The shrill sound of sirens wailed in the night sky, screeching to a stop in the street in front of their burning house.

Neighbors thronged to their yard, and one man took over the CPR on Allan.

Steve sat back in shock.

Maria clung to Sarah, holding her close. She could barely breathe, and she choked on smoke and tears that would not come. She noticed white-gray flakes sifted down like snow imbued with the smell of pain.

Blurred voices surrounded her, hands clasping and pulling, but she only held tighter, welded to the ground where she sat.

She mumbled, "…breathe baby, breathe…"

Steve's voice came from behind her. He reached for Sarah, "Maria, let them help her, please."

She turned, found his eyes, nodded, and tears streamed down her face. She released her grasp, skin peeling from her hands.

Maria fell into Steve's arms, and he held her until many hands pulled her up and laid her on a stretcher. A mask covered her face, and then darkness.

Steve jumped into an ambulance. Oblivious to the bubbles quickly forming on his hands and arms, he held Patrick and Lori close to him, and Jeffrey pressed at his side.

The doors slammed shut, and they lurched forward. Steve stared out the back window as they pulled away.

He fixated on the orange and yellow flames licking at the water in a hopeless attempt to drown the destructive hazard.

CHAPTER SIX

$\mathcal{S}$TEVE SAT in the reclining chair next to Maria's bed. The bells and monitors showed she was alive but wouldn't wake up.

His heart pounded; not knowing was agonizing. It pressed in him, choking him like the smoke the night before.

He didn't know anything; what to think or what to feel. His degrees, schooling, all these years of living, but right now, nothing made sense. He was scared.

The time was utterly irrelevant now. Steve wasn't sure if it had been minutes or hours, but he dozed off clutching Maria's bandaged arms, holding onto anything to keep him from sinking.

But sleep would not come. Instead, Steve's mind spun as he tried to sort through it.

Last night, when the ambulance arrived with Steve and their children, they were immediately rushed into separate rooms.

Doctors hurried in and out of Steve's room with the scorching smell of sanitizer mingling with the stench of smoke permeating from his skin and hair.

"Do you know anything about my children?"

A flurry of nurses, poking, prodding, blood draws.

More X-rays, oxygen, and blood draw.

"What's going on with my children?"

His anxiety and frustration only increased in their automatic responses.

"Let's just worry about you. Your family is in good hands."

"No! That's not good enough."

Steve's internal dialogue screamed inside his head. He tried to process what had happened to his family, but physically his body couldn't grasp it. Finally, he leaned forward, coughed, and struggled to breathe.

His reddened hands tingled, bubbles formed, and he started to feel the intense burn. He hadn't felt much before, and now he longed for the blessing of numbness.

With tenderness in her voice, one nurse finally asked. "Is there someone we can call for you?"

Steve nodded. "My mother," he whispered. Then, he closed his eyes and visualized how devastating this call would be for his mother.

Eventually, Steve was cleared of any "critical" injuries but ordered to be on oxygen and rest.

"Where are my children?" This time, though still weak, the strength of his demand finally connected with a nurse, who wheeled Steve into a room where Jeffrey and Patrick were.

He found Patrick sleeping in Jeffrey's arms, connected to monitors, wires, and oxygen. But he could see they were both okay, at least physically.

"Lori is just next door," said the nurse.

Her voice startled Steve. He had forgotten she was still behind him.

He nodded, and she gently guided him through the door and into the next room.

Tears immediately stung his burned cheeks. She looked small, alone, and lying so still and quiet. He suddenly thought the worst.

"Is she...?"

"Oh, no," the nurse assured him. "She's fine. She was so still; we were worried, too. But once we got her in there, one of our nurses held her until she fell asleep."

"And what about my Allan and Sarah?"

"I'm not sure yet. We moved both children to our specialty trauma center and haven't had an update in a while." Then, she smiled. "No news, good news, right?"

Or are you just saving my feelings?

Steve couldn't be sure if they were honest with him or protecting his feelings.

"My wife?" He struggled in a whisper.

"They're still stabilizing her. I'll take you to her as soon as we get her into a room."

Salty tears slowly leaked into the corner of his mouth, and Steve sighed.

He heard a light knock on the door and turned to face his mother.

The grief, worry, and pain were evident on her face.

Steve and his mother stared at each other silently. The nurse quietly slipped out of the room, and Steve collapsed into his mother's welcome arms.

The drive to the hospital seemed like an eternity to Lois.

It's Christmas! What were people doing out this early in the morning?

The last hour she played over in her head like a slow-motion movie. The phone call seemed so surreal.

The constant ringing had awakened her from a fitful sleep, but she didn't know why she had been so restless. As soon as she was alert, a knot formed in her stomach. A quick, silent prayer escaped her lips as she reached for the phone.

"Mrs. Marksworth?"

A sweet young voice broke through the white noise in the background.

"Yes, this is her."

"My name is Amanda Percival. I'm a nurse in the emergency room...."

Fire. Kids. Steve. Hospital. Could she come?

She had somehow managed to reply that she would be there as soon as possible, and she hung up the phone. Her body refused to move quickly; everything was a blur. She managed to dress, picked up her keys, and grabbed for her purse, but then stopped.

Lois stopped in the doorway and turned around. She scanned her living room; her eyes darted from one object to another, and suddenly things seemed unimportant.

Her heart pounded, and the weight of the phone call threatened to collapse her to the floor. She shuddered, and her head throbbed, but she felt an unseen strength come over her. She took a deep breath and hurried out the door while dabbing at tears that kept escaping. Lois made it to the hospital but couldn't remember how she got there. It was as if someone else was in control.

Lois tried to focus on what she was walking into. Right now, she needed to be strong for her son. She would deal with her feelings later.

CHAPTER SEVEN

SILENT, STILL WHITENESS. Emptiness all around her—opaque but blinding. Maria heard beeping, faint sounds, and mumbled voices. She wasn't sure and didn't care.

Wherever she was, she seemed to be nothing, with nothing; strangely, she felt nothing, which was okay.

Then, finally, a voice came through the whiteness. It sounded familiar, though different, but more mature.

Maria turned toward the voice. She could see faces, healthy beaming faces. But she wasn't sure who they were.

The distance to the faces felt so far, yet close simultaneously. There seemed to be a thin veil, a barrier of some kind. But the voice still called to Maria, and she yearned to go to them.

"Mommy! Wake up, Mommy!"

No, it's not time yet; let me rest a little longer. But I don't want this sweetness to go away.

"Mommy! Mommy!"

Maria forced her eyes to open slightly, only hazy light and beeping sounds.

She let her eyes drift closed as though it would stop the invasive sounds and smells of antiseptic and sulfur.

Suddenly feeling trapped, she tried to take a deep breath, but panic seized her; she tried to move, but a heaviness on her chest held her down.

She felt a familiar presence, and she turned toward it. Steve. She sighed. Things were coming into focus.

He was gently holding her arm. She was surrounded by blankets, bandages, and wires. Suddenly feeling claustrophobic, she couldn't breath and jerked her arm away.

Where are my kids?

She tried to say something, but her voice only cracked, and she gasped through the mask covering her face. She tried pulling it off but couldn't move her hands.

Steve pushed the call button. "She's awake!"

Immediately, a nurse came in and tried to calm Maria down.

"It's okay, Mrs. Marksworth. It's okay. I need you to calm down and hold still, please."

Jumbled images flashed through her mind. Heat, crying, flames; Maria tried to obey but couldn't concentrate.

Where are my kids?!

"I'm going to give you some medicine to help you, okay?"

The nurse turned to Steve, who nodded, and she quickly put the medicine into the tube.

A wave of calm enveloped her. Her eyes closed again, and the whiteness returned.

"Mommy! I love you, Mommy!"

I love you, too.

Silence.

Steve stalked the hallways between the children's rooms and Maria's for several hours.

He was supposed to be in his room resting, but he couldn't sit still, so the nurses equipped him with an oxygen tank on wheels.

Steve and his mother took turns staying with Maria and the kids. Finally, he found time to call her parents, and now they were on their way.

He sat beside Maria's bed wondering how a few days could feel like years.

His sorrow seemed endless. How did my mom do it?

Maria was regularly given pain meds for her burns and slept most of the time; her lungs were of grave concern as well.

She stirred slightly this time, slowly coming out of the drugs. The concern for her.

Steve rubbed his temples. The tubes coming out of her were hard to look at.

Her eyes fluttered, then slowly opened.

"Maria, sweetie, it's me. You're doing okay." He tried to reassure her.

He was relieved that she seemed a little calmer now.

Her whisper seemed forced. "Steve, the kids. Where are the kids?"

He choked on the words. "They're sleeping; Mom's with them. They're being taken care of. Just rest."

How can I tell her?

He didn't even believe it himself. He couldn't say anything, and he couldn't breathe. Tears streamed down his face.

"Please, where are the kids?" Suddenly, she seemed to focus and turned and looked at her husband. She had never seen him cry like this.

Pain racked every muscle and bone in his body. He finally returned her gaze, and they found each other's eyes brimming with tears. Anguish overtook him—he buried his face in his hands and cried bitterly.

CHAPTER EIGHT

*A*DOCTOR GENTLY KNOCKED on the glass pane, then stepped inside the room.

"Hi, Mr. and Mrs. Marksworth? I'm Dr. Kane, an internist here in the ICU."

Steve nodded and managed a quiet, "Yes."

Maria nodded.

"I know it's been a rough few days, and I'm so sorry to say it won't get easier soon. Both of you have some lung damage from the smoke. Maria, your lungs are considerably worse. In addition, the third-degree burns on your hands and the heat damage on your legs have caused severe swelling."

Steve's heart sank to depths he didn't know possible. "What does all of that mean?"

Dr. Kane hesitated. "Two main concerns; infection and decreased mobility, which could be permanent."

Steve looked at the floor. Why did it have to be her?

He took a deep breath as sickness washed over him like a tidal wave. Acid crept into his throat and lingered; he swallowed before it could escape. He tried to focus on what the doctor was saying.

Maria rasped, "…. my kids."

Dr. Kane's countenance changed, and evident sadness filled his clouded eyes. Then, finally, he cleared his throat. "Lori and Jeffrey are okay. Minor smoke inhalation, but they are good. Patrick must stay on oxygen for another day or so for observation. Luckily, they were on bottom bunks."

Maria glanced at Steve, and he nodded.

Patrick and Allan usually slept on the top bunk, Jeffrey on the bottom. That bed creaked like an old boat, so how they had made their way out of bed without either hearing them was beyond Steve.

Silence hung in the room.

Maria muttered, "Sarah? Allan?"

Steve squeezed her arm above the bandages. He had known for a few days, but he still hadn't processed the news and couldn't bring himself to tell Maria. He worried about her reaction.

Finally, Dr. Kane said, "I'm sorry. We tried to revive them for over an hour. Too much toxin…. smoke…. too much…."

Steve barely heard what Dr. Kane was saying. He stared at Maria; her face was blank.

Maria tried to breathe, think, and reason, but nothing materialized.

She became aware of another body in the room, Steve reaching for her hand and then white open plains filled with light again.

She drifted to sleep but forced her eyes open again.

Lois was next to her.

"Hi there, sweetie, it's okay, I'm here."

Her mother-in-law's voice soothed the edges of the pain tearing at her insides.

"Steve went to settle the kids, and then he'll be back."

Maria nodded and wished she could see and hold them with her there in her own bed. Her arms ached, and she attempted to shift in her bed. Nausea and searing pain hit her all at once. She wanted to fall back into oblivion again.

A nurse entered, checked Maria's vitals, made some notes on a chart, and left.

Dr. Kane came in with another nurse. "Maria, it's nice to see you awake again."

Maria didn't respond. Her throat burned, and breathing made her choke.

Steve came in, shook the doctor's hand, and sat on the edge of Maria's bed.

"I am so, so sorry for your loss, I can't even imagine." Dr. Kane paused. "We would like to give you some time to hold your children if you would like to. It can be hard, but we can offer it, if you feel like you can."

The nurse said quietly, "We will wrap them in blankets, and you can hold them as long as you want. I've seen it help families say goodbye, but if it's too much, that's okay, too. There is no pressure."

There was something in her voice that was reassuring to Maria.

Maria turned to Steve; he was looking at her. She turned away, unable to meet his gaze any longer for fear of completely breaking down. She nodded, but she didn't look at the doctor or at Steve.

She heard Steve mutter, "Okay."

She heard Dr. Kane giving instructions to the nurse as they left the room. The sound of their voices soon drifted away.

Maria's heart pounded, and her insides filled with butterflies.

It was just like when she gave birth to them, not knowing what was coming, what it would be like, and how she would cope. Wonder and awe had awaited her then. Now, she feared what was coming. It wasn't real, it simply couldn't be.

Steve attempted to swallow the lump that formed in his throat, but the constant taste of ash and soap choked him. The acidic bile still continued to swell into a rancid taste in his mouth, but nothing burned more than the growing emptiness he felt.

He ached to hold his children, but not to face the reality he knew was coming for Maria and him.

For now, he could still argue with himself it wasn't real, pretend the lifeless bodies he had tried to revive were smiling and laughing in another room.

The nurse returned, removed some of the wires, straightened the bed, and helped Maria to sit up. Steve sat in a chair next to her.

It wasn't long before two nurses entered the room, each carrying a carefully wrapped bundle. A nurse carefully placed Sarah in Steve's arms. He turned and gently handed her to Maria. It felt like a deep hole ripped through his heart when he turned to receive Allan from the other nurse.

Trembling, he sat on the bed next to Maria. His mind raced back to the day the twins were born, this was much like that day. Only now, they were alone in their pained sobs, holding their two silent babies.

They looked like they were sleeping. Still and slightly pink, but cold, empty shells. Dr. Kane had prepared them for this. It was the Co2.

Maria put Sarah to her chest, humming as she rocked back and forth. She seemed smaller than normal, and unnaturally quiet. Lifeless. The emptiness penetrated Maria's soul.

Steve stared into his son's face searching for something, anything, from the day before. Squeals, laughter, and silliness; all gone. Unlike the day he was born, he was limp, silent.

Loss and heartache pumped through every beat of Steve's heart.

How can I still be alive with all this pain inside me?

He pulled Allan closer, and sobs shook his body.

Maria looked at him, at her son, then down at her daughter. Something inside of her snapped and uncontrollable sobs seized her, but still she held onto the tiny form with all she had.

CHAPTER NINE

*M*ARIA DIDN'T OPEN HER EYES. The haunting voices still called to her. But now, she could see their faces. Sarah, healthy and walking, older than she should be, and hand-in-hand with a sad but vibrant Allan.

Together, their sweet voices pierced her without sound. "Mommy! Mommy! I love you, Mommy!"

The harsh icy truth was growing where the hole had burned inside her heart, and the dread that she would awake to nothingness.

Maria drifted into sleep again. Steve sank into the reclining chair and wondered what they would do now. The entirety of their situation weighed on him like a sinking ship.

Like the day when he met Maria and discovered that God must be honest, but now, he knew there could be no God. How could a God take his children from them? What benevolence is there that would allow this?

And yet, when he closed his eyes, he saw his father with his two children, who were alive and happy. Could there be something after this life? No, just a fanciful dream trying to comfort him. He closed his eyes and tried to breathe.

Whenever he dreamed of his children, he saw them playing and full of life. Their giggles, their movements and joy were so real.

He felt a light touch on his arm. He opened his eyes, and he realized he was crying. Lori was standing next to him with her hand on his arm.

"Daddy, are you okay?"

"Yes, sweetie. Now that you're here."

Lori climbed onto Steve's lap. He put his arm around her, and she snuggled in close.

Lois walked in, holding Jeffrey's and Patrick's hands. She pulled a chair beside Maria's bed and lifted Patrick onto her lap. Jeffrey sat in another chair next to his mother's bed.

Steve noticed Jeffrey looked at Maria, but she turned away from them. Tears leaked from Jeffrey's eyes. Steve reached over and patted his leg.

A nurse walked in, pushing a breakfast cart.

She put a plate on the bed tray and rolled it before Maria. "You need to eat something."

Maria didn't acknowledge her presence.

No one seemed to be hungry, not even the kids.

Lois eyed her daughter-in-law and felt the ache of her loss. But she knew this had to be more significant for her losing two children simultaneously. Even now, her arms and heart ached at the possibility and remembrance of years ago.

She helped Lori with her plate while Steve tried to coax

Patrick to eat. Jeffrey moved food around on his plate, but he didn't eat much.

The silence was deafening. Lois finally turned to Steve.

"Your brothers will be here tomorrow, Steve. They had to get things together before they flew in."

He didn't respond.

She continued. "I don't want you two to worry about the funeral arrangements. Maria's parents and I will take care of everything, but we will do whatever you want."

Lois looked at Maria. Lois hoped that by taking this on, it would alleviate some of the pressure. Maybe, then Maria might come back to them, if only for a moment.

But she didn't.

Steve glanced at Maria and then at his mom. Then, at length, he said, "Something small, just a graveside, okay?"

"That's fine, whatever you want." Lois smiled faintly and then looked at Maria, and the creases in her forehead deepened. Lois wanted to reach out and hold Maria with her whole being, but she didn't even know if that Could comfort her.

Maria's parents had been helping with the children, so Lois could go home and get some rest.

Rest. That was impossible. Whenever Lois's eyes closed, she felt sorrow and guilt that she couldn't do anything. All her years of living and nothing had prepared her for this, not even the death of her husband.

She looked at photos, thinking of him and the cold, harsh reality that awaited her son and Maria in their new world without their children. Now, watching them, she knew the road ahead would be rough, and they hoped they would survive it together.

Chapter Ten

$\mathcal{A}$ FTER THE NURSES had cleared their trays and the children laid down again, Lois went to call Maria's parents.

Even though they had not been close to Maria since her decision to marry Steve, Lois was in hopes of making some arrangements with them.

Initially, it seemed as if they would disown their daughter completely, but they began to come around after Jeffery was born. They made a trip about once a year from Southern California for a visit.

Maria had often talked to Lois about her relationship with her parents, and Lois had tried to help fill the void and become more than just a mother-in-law to her.

Now, she felt sorry for them. They did not get to know their grandchildren as well as she had and had missed out on so many precious memories.

None of that would help right now, though. Lois knew this could be a touchy time between Maria and her parents, but she hoped that maybe this tragedy, in some strange way, could help bring them together again.

Dr. Kane made his rounds and came in to check on the family.

"Well, at least some good news for the moment. Steve, you and the kids are ready to be discharged today. Maria, your hands are healing better than we thought, but they are still a concern, and your legs are going to require a lot more healing time. The damage to your lungs is going to take a while to heal as well."

He paused as though expecting some questions. When none came, he continued. "We'll transfer you down to a medical floor and watch you carefully for another day or so. We will also keep you on oxygen for a while, even after you go home. The physical things are going to take time, along with the emotional and mental healing."

Maria just turned away and closed her eyes.

Steve stared at her momentarily, then looked back at the doctor.

"I'm sorry for your loss. I wish there was more we could do," said Dr. Kane.

There was no pity in his face, and Steve said, "We're grateful for all you've been able to do. Really."

He meant it; despite all his pain, he knew it could be much worse.

Dr. Kane looked at Maria and back to Steve, nodded, and left the room.

Lois returned to find Steve staring at the corner of the ceiling. He jumped a little when she came in.

Maria was still asleep, so she lowered her voice.

"I'm sorry. I didn't mean to scare you, dear." She leaned over and touched his arm. "I passed a nurse in the hall with the kids. Is she taking them to the play area?"

"Yeah, she is, and that's okay, Mom. I was just thinking." He sighed. "I'll get up later, but right now, I don't want to move at all."

Steve was exhausted; physically, emotionally, and mentally. His entire being just felt tired. He looked at her as she pulled up a chair. "Mom?"

"Yes, son?" She sat down and leaned forward, so she could hear him closely. He still mainly whispered, and her hearing wasn't what it used to be.

"What are we going to do? Where are we going to go?"

She heard his words; tension, worry, and pain. His drawn face struggled so hard to keep composure.

"They are sending some social worker around to help us decide what to do, but honestly, I don't even have a clue or know what arrangements there are to be made. Where do we even start?"

The reality of loss flowed out now. "We have nothing. We don't have any clothes, possessions, nothing."

His composure cracked. "Mom, we don't even have all of our family anymore." He stuttered on these last words, and tears flowed freely down his cheeks.

Lois was crying, too. She held his hand and wiped his tears like she had when he was little.

After a few moments, when they had both stopped crying, and they sat in silence, Lois said matter-of-factly, "What do you mean you don't have anywhere to go? You will come home with me until we can rebuild yours or find you something else. You can stay there as long as you need. It's way too large for one older woman, anyway. As for the rest, we will take care of that as we go."

His mother sat there with such determination and resolve that Steve managed a slight smile and wondered how he ever could have doubted what he would do.

Of course, they would move in with her. They didn't have much, but they were still a family. They would deal with the rest as it came.

Just then, the nurse walked in. "Excuse me, but some young people are here to see you. I have them in the conference room if you want to go in there so as not to disturb your wife?"

Steve's eyebrows furrowed, and he looked at his mother.

She looked back with the same puzzled expression.

"Sure." He straightened up as much as he could before gingerly getting up.

He and Lois walked into the conference room to find over half a dozen of his students with large garbage bags in tow.

Steve looked into their faces, then again at the garbage bags. "What's this?"

Robert Basset, from Steve's third-period language studies, nervously looked around at the others and then walked forward.

The muscular, five-foot-eleven football player with light brown hair stood awkwardly before the group. His strong jawline softened around his clouded eyes. Robert was a good student when he wasn't cracking jokes or talking about a game; today, he was doing neither.

Robert cleared his throat. "Well, Mr. Marksworth, we heard that your family was in a fire the other night. So, with the help of our parents, we got together and were able to get some things that we hope might help you out."

He picked up a couple of bags, and others started passing them forward. They were all so somber that Steve had a hard time believing these were the same students who pulled practical jokes weekly in his classroom.

"We have clothes for your kids. We also got some clothes for you and your wife," said Robert; he pulled some out to prove that they had accomplished what they said.

A young lady piped up from behind. "We love you, Mr. Marksworth."

Others then chimed in, overlapping each other, "We're praying for you."

"Get better soon."

"We're hoping the best."

Lois fondly hugged Robert, who stood beside her. She released him and scanned all of their faces.

"Thank you all so much."

Lois took a moment to thank each one and at least shake their hand, touch their arm, or shoulder.

The young lady from the back looked past Lois at Steve and caught his eyes. "We really do love you, Mr. Marksworth. We'll be praying for your family."

She was so sincere, so honest.

Steve couldn't speak; she seemed somehow to understand.

They both looked in disbelief as they saw brand-new clothes with tags still on them, along with others that were probably used but still in good repair.

Steve lowered himself into a chair. He was visibly shocked and overcome with awe and gratitude.

Lois rested her hand reassuringly on his shoulder.

Robert hurriedly added as if he needed to explain more. "We kept the tags on these so that you could exchange them for different sizes if they don't fit.

"As soon as you know where you will be going, we also have other things to bring you, if that's okay?" His face strained with anxiety, and he seemed to be waiting for a hint of approval from their teacher.

Steve smiled, and tears threatened at the corners of his eyes. "Robert… everyone, this is the most wonderful thing you could have ever done for us. You don't know what this means to me and my family."

The kids awkwardly stared at their feet, but their eyes sparkled, and smiles spread across their faces.

Lois fondly hugged this boy again, who had done so much for her son.

Robert blushed, mumbled something, and handed Steve a card with his mom's phone number on it, and then led them all out again. Lois turned back to her son, who was watching them go with a smile on his tired face.

That evening, once the children had finally gone to sleep, Steve sat next to Maria. She had eaten better that evening, but she still hadn't spoken. She had held Patrick all evening until her arms could no longer support his weight. Then she curled her knees up as far as the swelling would allow and stared off again.

He avoided touching her arms as they were increasingly sore. Placing his good hand on her face, he tried to reach her.

"Maria. Maria, please! Tell me, what is going on? What are you feeling? I can only help if you open up to me. I need you! I need you here with the kids. I need you with me. Please, just say something."

She turned and looked at him with tears leaking from the corners of her eyes. Everything in her wanted to scream, shout, and cry; anything. But something in her just wouldn't let it happen.

"I can't," she managed to whisper. Then the sobs came. She pulled him to her and buried her head in his chest. His smell, his strength, and his tenderness all filled her senses.

Still, he couldn't fill her longing arms or the emptiness in her heart. He could not erase their pleading faces every time she closed her eyes. She could hear their voices in her mind. She felt as if she were being punished for something.

While growing up, Maria understood that there was life after this and that you could be saved by grace alone. All one must do is proclaim belief, and you will be saved. Maria had questioned this. She rejected it. She had wanted to know, for herself, if it was right. The pastor and her parents had argued with her for hours. What could she possibly disagree with?

Was this her punishment for turning away from all of this? Did she not have enough faith? They also taught that there wouldn't be families like we are now. That all bonds were broken at death. What good was life after this if you didn't stay with the ones you loved? The words of the pastor echoed painfully through her.

"Well, of course, you do," the pastor had argued, "you won't just have family units anymore. We are all there together as separate entities to enjoy paradise."

To Marie, it was horrible torture, the true fire and brimstone that further widened the gaping hole inside of her soul, and she felt the cruelty even more deeply. It couldn't be right to allow us to have families, feel such love, and not be family anymore. That didn't make sense. She continued attending church to please her parents until she moved out to go to school. They had all but disowned her when she married Steve and announced they would not be attending any church.

This idea may seem like a happy end to her parents, just going into heaven, with no ties, etc. But these were hollow promises in this moment, in this pain, in this loss. She wanted her children to be hers, and she didn't want any part of a God that would make this his punishment for her lack of faith.

But even Lois couldn't answer her questions, and Maria had given up on getting any explanation at all. Nothing was certain in this life, and she had accepted that fact until now.

This was different. She needed something to hold on to, and there was nothing there. She felt like she was falling, and nothing was there to catch her. She would fall forever, never landing.

CHAPTER ELEVEN

*T*HE FIREFIGHTERS had worked for hours to try to contain the blaze, but the house was so old and small that everything was combusted, shooting out sparks that only fueled the fire. They knew they had to let the embers slowly finish burning, wetting down the surrounding areas to keep it from spreading again.

The fire marshall's report, clinical, cold, and devoid of life, read "Electrical failure in the walls of the aging trailer home."

Maria was finally well enough to be released from the hospital. The day was unreasonably and unseasonably cold and still.

Nurses packed her into a wheelchair, gently arranging her bandaged hands and arms to minimize bumping and jarring. The oxygen tank was nestled into its slot, tethered to her face by the clear plastic tubing.

It seemed like a lifetime in that room, and Maria feared what was next.

A nurse handed the bag of bottles and papers to Steve, who put them into the large plastic bag of her other hospital-acquired things.

"Here are the orders and the medication schedule," said the nurse. "And don't forget that she will need to do her exercises at least three times a day. A nurse will come in and do Maria's required bandage changes. Also, her primary care physician's office will be in touch...."

Steve's head was spinning. The instructions seemed to go on forever. How would he ever remember all of it?

Finally, they reached the first floor. Maria was wheeled to the front hospital doors, and then they paused for the nurse to double-check everything.

Steve looked at Maria and then at the doors and felt fear at the uncertainty before him.

The children were already waiting in the car and peeked their heads out. Seeing them gave him strength and resolve as they moved forward.

Now, as the family looked upon the burnt shambles of their precious home, the reality hit them. It was gone. Only ashes remained, softly blowing in the breeze of the cool December air. Soon authorities would scoop it up and take it to a dump. That is where their lives would end up. Out there, buried and alone with nothing left to recognize. Nothing to show it was once a happy home and family.

Silently, Maria stared at the ashes and saw it all vividly in her mind. The flames, the smoke, the still lifeless bodies. Only now, it came in slow motion instead of the flashes that seemed to be burned into her brain.

Time seemed only to go on forever, replaying it over and over. Her family of seven was now only five, and the loss of the two little ones was unbearable to her.

How could this happen? It had been Christmas, for heaven's sake! They didn't have much, but what they had was enough for them. Now, what was there?

Steve couldn't get the beautiful faces of their lost little ones or the glow of the embers out of his heart and mind.

They were only three and five. Why? Just why? persisted in his mind. Yet the clock's hands still moved forward. Life went on despite them, without them, and haunted his dreams. How would they ever rebuild? Can they rebuild?

Certainly… there is no such thing.

Then the anger engulfed him, and he fought against his pain!

The ever-growing ache burned within both of them like the fire leaving an empty space in their hearts.

They knew people who would judge, who would look at them and never speak the words. Only their eyes would say it all. Would it ever end? How would they ever go on?

Unable to take anymore, Maria turned away. She walked gingerly the few steps back to the car.

Steve followed her with the children. He watched her and wondered if she would ever speak to him again if she would ever recover. Could he even really expect that of her? He would give her time and love and hope that would be enough.

It had worked for his mother.

He also knew Maria would never be the same again, and neither would he. He hoped that, in the end, they would be able to come together again in a way stronger than before. But for now, he would just wait.

When Steve and the children were discharged, they refused to leave the hospital until Maria could leave with them a few days later. Their first stop was their house.

The therapist had suggested it as a way to process the reality, and Steve hoped they would be right, but Maria only slipped further into the wish for oblivion.

When they arrived at Lois's house later in the afternoon, they were greeted by several cars parked out front, and people waiting on the steps and front lawn. Who were these people? Why would they be here and now?

Steve got out first and started helping the children out.

Maria couldn't quite walk very far yet without great pain, so Lois retrieved the wheelchair from the trunk.

As Steve, Jeffrey, Lori, and Patrick approached the house, he recognized some of these people as parents of his current students but also parents of past students. He wondered why they would come. Then others he didn't know at all.

Robert's mother approached him first. She was the complete opposite of her son. White, blond hair and a mere four foot five inches tall, with a fair complexion and tiny frame. With pixie features and a voice that was like a singing bird.

"Mr. Marksworth." She offered her hand and then seemed to notice the wrap, and she quickly waved past him to Maria. "Mrs. Marksworth."

Steve's forehead was beginning to furrow, and the lump, which had begun to leave his throat, made its way back. "Mrs. Basset, how can I help you?"

"The question is more of how may we help you? We have brought more clothes and some groceries that hopefully will get you all through the weekend. We needed to determine your preferences, so we only got the basics. Later, we can get a list together, so we can plan out better for you. Also, we found some more things that you could use. My husband is bringing some beds over for the children if you can use them?"

It wasn't a question; she merely continued. "Also, we have had an offer of a queen bed for you and your wife if you want it."

She paused for a moment. There was no reply, and she continued slowly. "So if you or your mother would like to show us where to put these, we'll get things started."

Steve was speechless. Searching their faces, he found concern, not pity. Each one looked on as though hoping to find a way to help his family.

Lois came from behind and pushed Maria's wheelchair next to him.

Lois smiled. "Please forgive my son." She patted his arm. "For a teacher, he can often run short on words." She took Mrs. Basset by the arm and made her way through the crowd of women and youth holding boxes and bags.

A woman walked over to Jeffrey, Patrick, and Lori.

"Hi, guys. My name is Holly. I have something in this box that I think you guys would really like."

They looked up to Steve and Maria for consent.

Their parents nodded, and their eager eyes told Holly the answer.

She opened the box. Inside were cars, trucks, blocks, Lego's, and an assortment of other toys. Patrick, Lori, and Jeffery tentatively stared at the assortment. After looking back up, seeking confirmation that these were now theirs, the boys cried out in joy, each grabbing a toy to carry into the house. Lori timidly looked up with her big eyes and asked, "Do you have any dolls?"

Holly grinned and pulled a life-size baby doll from behind her back. The doll had golden hair, rosy cheeks, and had on a beautiful dress and shiny slippers.

"I was hoping you'd say that," said Holly. "This little one needs a home really bad. Do you think you could love her and take care of her?"

Lori's head had never nodded so fast in her whole life. Her eyes grew even wider when she took the doll into her arms, cradled it, and rocked it back and forth as she carried it into the house.

Once inside, Holly gave her a bag with several more dresses, blankets, and a baby bottle.

Lori grabbed her around the neck and held on tight. "Thank you!" She whispered it, but the whole room seemed to feel the sweet gentleness and love this child had just given.

Holly's eyes filled with tears. "You are most welcome."

She then spoke to Mrs. Basset, "Sister Basset, I think I'm going to leave now. The children are home alone with Jason, and I don't know how long he can handle them."

Mrs. Basset smiled at her in understanding and nodded.

Holly walked away but then turned back.

Lori was still watching her. She smiled and then left.

"You have a new friend," Lois said to Lori.

Lori took her doll to the room they had always stayed in when they came to visit. The boys followed with their box of toys.

Steve was still in shock.

As they entered the house and set Maria up in the recliner, he observed the women swiftly taking to work. Quietly and in order, working easily and swiftly together.

Lois showed them to the kitchen, and then they took over. Some of them unwrapping dishes that were already prepared and putting them in the oven. Others set the table, and the rest put away the groceries.

Steve watched in wonder. Who were these women? Who would come and do this for his family? They couldn't all be parents, many of them couldn't even be more than twenty years old.

They finished in little more than half an hour, and most of them started leaving with nods and a quick goodbye. Some of them, mostly the ones he had known, stopped to pay their respects, and asked if there was anything else they could do. He told them he didn't think so, and then they left.

In the end, only Mrs. Basset remained. She seemed a little frustrated. "I can't imagine where my husband could be right now. Robert has practice soon, and we were trying not to go too much on that."

She moved the curtain and peeked outside. "Finally," she murmured. She opened the door, gave some instructions, and stepped out of the way.

In walked a big burly man of about six foot three and thick around.... well, everywhere.

His beard reached the middle of his chest, and his dark hair was speckled with gray strands. One end of a mattress was on his shoulder, still in a plastic covering.

He grunted hello as he passed and kept going; Robert carried the other end, wearing his football uniform.

Two uniformed football players carried in another. They made another trip for bed frames.

Steve heard clinging and bangs coming from the room above them as they deftly assembled the beds.

This whole time Maria sat quietly, taking it all in. She didn't know any of these people. In fact, she was even a little angry with them for doing what she could not. Even more so, she was angry with herself for not being able to show gratitude for their service. To thank them for giving so freely of themselves at this time to complete strangers.

As she listened to the building of the beds in the other room, she also heard the awe of her boys as they asked question after question of these men about how and what they were doing.

The replies were soft and gentle, always brief but satisfying the childish wonder inside of them. She looked at her bandaged hands and sniffled.

Why can't I make myself do what I need to do? Why can't I be there for my children? Here I sit, and they are getting the attention they need from complete strangers! What good am I right now, though? I can't even speak to them or my husband.

She reclined the chair, pulled the blanket on her lap up to her chin, and closed her eyes, trying to block the anger growing inside her.

About thirty minutes later, the boys left, quickly saying they would stay but that they had practice. Steve smiled and thanked them.

Mrs. Basset, however, stayed behind talking to Lois. Steve could see they were making out a list. He couldn't hear everything, but he made out an acceptance for the other bed. Mrs. Basset said it would be by tomorrow and then came over to Steve.

"Mr. Marksworth, I would really like to say how sorry I am for what you are going through. I know nothing I can say or do will take away the hurt right now. But we would all like to help if we can. If there is anything you need, please don't hesitate to call. I left my number with your mother, okay?"

She was sitting across from him and looking at him straight on. She was sincere in her voice, and he knew she meant it.

"Why?" he asked. "Why are you all doing this for us? You hardly know us." His face showed admiration and also wonder at this woman and all she'd done.

"Well, sir, that's just what we do when someone needs it. I'm only sorry we didn't know before all of this what we could have done to help you. That won't happen again. We should have become friends with your family a long time ago. Sometimes it takes things like this to make you realize how unimportant some of the things in your own life are and how much you are needed doing other things. I know it has for us. I've never seen Robert so selfless and helpful in all his life. You have been a big influence on him, and he never quite knew how to tell you that. Doing this for your family is his way of saying it now. Please, don't forget you are not alone. Okay?"

By this time, Steve was speechless and felt the hot burning in his eyes again. Although her eyes were shut, Maria had heard it all as well. Something in this woman's voice was calming and peaceful. So assured of her place. Both of them inwardly hoped that they could have this feeling last. Something was stirring, and they didn't quite know what it was, but this stranger had brought some peace into this house, and they never wanted it to leave.

And when she left, the feeling lingered.

CHAPTER TWELVE

***M**ARIA STOOD BY THE DOOR* looking in on her children, listening to what they were saying, as they hadn't seen her yet. Patrick was asking Lori if she thought Allan was okay. "Did he go to heaven to be with Jesus like Granny said?"

"I guess so. I don't think he's alone. I think he's got Sarah and Grandpa Marksworth with him wherever he is."

Her answer was so straightforward and honest. So sure, and simple. Maria wished she had even just that simple knowledge right now, that they were safe, somewhere, not just cold in a box.

"Why doesn't Mommy or Daddy know where they are?" she heard Patrick ask.

Maria cringed. His innocence didn't allow for the ability of no answers to questions in life. Oh, how she wished she had answers, any answers.

At that thought, she turned, slumped, and curled up into a ball. There was nothing left to feel. Nothing left to attempt to understand. All there was, was darkness engulfing what there used to be of her soul. Nothingness is all that she felt and saw before her now.

The next morning came too early and cold.

Maria's parents arrived from their hotel early in the morning and spent the time helping Lois get the children ready.

Steve's brothers had come by the house before and said they would meet them at the graveside.

So, Steve and Maria spent a few moments alone, sitting on the newly acquired bed and staring at the closet.

"I guess we should get ready then, huh?" Steve was unsure why he even said it. The words sounded foreign and distant even to his own ears.

Maria just stared off, not moving.

Steve stood up, opened the closet, and pulled out the suit his students brought for him.

He also pulled out a black skirt and sweater blouse for Maria; when she didn't reach for it, he laid it next to her. She just sat there. He knelt at her feet, helpless and weak, and gently took her hand.

Then he leaned in and tried to look in her eyes, but she diverted them.

"Maria, please! Please just say something. I'm worried about you. The kids, they need you. I know it hurts. I hurt. They are hurting, too. But I can only do this with you. Please!"

He hoped something he said would reach her, but she only gingerly pulled her hand away, awkwardly got up, and scuffled to the bathroom to change.

Still crouched, Steve hung his head, hoping against hope that somehow she would eventually come back to him.

But there was nothing in return.

When they eventually came down, Maria heard her parents talking to Lois.

"I wish she'd only have stayed in the church. Then maybe this wouldn't be so hard on her." Her mother had a high-pitched, harsh voice that seemed critical even when giving a compliment.

Her father piped in next with his deep tenor voice.

"Now, now. She made her choice. I wish that we were holding some kind of service in a church, so the children could get something out of it."

Lois came to their defense. "This is what they wanted, so this is what they get. Besides, the children are handling this pretty well considering everything. We've had some great talks, and they know that their brother and sister are okay. I think that maybe we should just let them handle this in their own way, as it is their family."

The emphasis on "their," with the tone of finality, was typical of Lois.

She had effectively shut them down, in the way she always had with them when they started in like this. Maria was grateful to her but was still hurt by her parents' criticism. She already blamed herself. She was already struggling with her own guilt and insecurities, and now this.

She had expected the backbiting, the whispering, and the pity from others, but not from her parents. She had hoped that they might be a little more sympathetic.

As she and Steve entered the room, her parents looked down and then up again as if changing characters in a play. They coddled and fawned over her, and Maria simply tolerated it.

Steve knew they meant well, but also how much this was hurting his wife on top of all the other agony she was already going through. He admired her for keeping her composure but, at the same time, wished that she would scream out at them, let loose some of the anguish and pain that was eating away inside her. That he could handle. But not knowing what she was thinking, feeling, or going through was harder for him to cope with. This interminable silence worried him.

"It's time to go, everyone," said Steve. With a pained face, he slowly moved between the children an held his tender hands out to them.

Patrick and Lori took hold of Steve's hands, and Jeffrey moved to stand at Maria's side. Steve took a moment to gaze at each of them, heaved a sigh, and led them to the car.

Maria didn't even look down at him. She knew if she did, it would only deepen the well within her. The wall she was building to protect and keep that hole at bay was still cementing, and she was afraid of it crumbling around her and exposing her weakness, failure, and pain.

When they pulled into the cemetery, Steve saw his brothers and their wives standing in a huddle talking.

At the sound of the cars pulling in, they stopped and turned to face Steve and his family. He hardly knew his brothers anymore, let alone their families. The distance between them made them seem like outsiders looking in on his shattered world. Still, he was grateful that they would come and was determined that he would do more to become closer to them himself. He knew family was important but never thought how much he had allowed everyday life to keep him at bay as well. Right then, he determined that he needed to do better. He resolved to at least try.

They gathered around the caskets, which were already set up over the open ground.

Steve and Lois sat on either side of Maria. A special chair had been provided for her. She shuddered but remained stone-faced and unmoving. Jeffrey stood stoically at her side. Lori crawled into Lois' lap, and Patrick allowed Steve to pull him into his arms.

A local priest who worked for the mortuary said a few words, which fell into the air and blew away. All she saw were her children, cold and lifeless, put into the cold, uncaring ground.

This is it. No more running into her while she cooked. No more loud crashes from the room or giggles at night while he and his brother spoke to each other in words only they knew. No more big eyes staring up at her for help, and no more long nights holding her in the rocker while the bouts of coughing took over her. But most of all, there would be no more laughter, no smiles to greet her mornings, no little scrapes and hurts to kiss away. Tears were now running down Maria's face, but she made no attempt to wipe them away. She stayed put, just staring at the two carved boxes, which now cradled her babies.

Steve, too, did not hear the words the priest spoke. His mind reflected on the moments he held the children in his arms after Maria gave birth. They had been so small and helpless. They depended so much upon him, and he had failed. How would he ever live without his precious angel or his wild little man in his life?

But he knew that life would go on because it did when his dad died. He knew each day would pass, and that life would eventually go on. But what peace was in that if, in the end, there was nothing left of his family to hold on to?

At that moment, he decided that there must be a life after this, or none of it made any sense. But still, what was it? Is this the truth he was meant to find? Is this what Sarah and Allan were trying to tell him in his dreams?

He shook his head and held Patrick and Lori even more tightly to him. Jeffrey still stood next to Maria and without any prompting put his arm around her shoulder.

Maria looked at her oldest child briefly and saw no longer a child but all the pain of a grown man in his eyes. She put her arm around Jeffrey's waist and pulled him into her. She could at least do that.

As Lois stood by the gaping holes, memories of her dear husband and his sudden death flooded over her. All the years without him had been hard, but as she gazed at her son and the caskets holding his children, she knew deep within that he was there with these precious children, waiting for the rest of them to join them.

She watched her daughter-in-law's parents whisper and converse throughout. She felt sorry that they didn't get the chance to know these wonderful children. She wasn't quite sure what they believed about death and the hereafter, but she knew it wasn't helpful to shame them or force anything. That never did any good for anyone. She herself knew that the children were still themselves with all the beauty of their personalities and loving hearts. No religion had taught her this; she had just always known. She held onto this with all she had when her husband died, and now it gave her hope that she would one day see him and her grandchildren again.

Before Steve guided the car away from the graves, he and Maria held Jeffrey, Patrick, and Lori tightly, and they all cried.

Patrick whispered something as he looked out the window, which Maria knew was in his private twin language, and she hoped that Allan was hearing.

Lori held onto the doll that had been given to her. She kept singing a lullaby like she had to Sarah on nights that were hard on her.

Steve let Jeffrey lay his head on his chest, and he felt the heat of tears dripping through the linen. This was the first time he'd seen him cry since the fire. He knew it would help him begin to heal and held him even closer, knowing what it meant to grow up too fast, and how this would change who he was and would become.

CHAPTER THIRTEEN

ITHIN THE NEXT WEEK, Maria's parents left.

"We just don't know what else we can do," her mother said.

However, the women who had come the first day they returned home came in little groups bearing more food and offers of assistance.

Children came with donated bedding, dolls, and other toys, often personally handing them to the kids. Steve watched as little ones no older than three or four years handed over gifts and smiled when Grandma Lois invited them to come by and play for a while and to come back often if they wanted to.

All this while Maria sat in a chair in the living room, staring out the window. She never spoke and ate very little. He was sure her hands and legs were part of what was causing her to act the way she did, but while she slept, Steve could hear her crying and talking to herself.

Over and over, he asked, pleaded, even chided some days, but she only turned away from him, often even staying in the chair to sleep. The children tried to get her to do things with them, but she would look at them and then away as if it hurt her to see them standing in front of her.

Her silence was starting to impact them all. They weren't sure what was wrong; did she blame herself? Did she blame him? What did she see when she saw their faces that kept her from looking?

Answers never came, and the gulf only grew wider.

Early one morning, after Jeffrey was ready for school, Steve saw him standing at the door to their room, looking at his mom. Steve wondered what that young brain was avidly thinking, his face twisted and eyes intent. At first, Jeffrey was quiet and unsure, but Steve knew his son, so he didn't let up.

Crouching to his level, he prodded. "Come on, tell me. It could help, buddy." His face and mouth pursed in great concern for his boy. He knew the consequences of holding things inside and didn't want his son to follow in his footsteps.

Finally, Jeffrey blurted out, "Why is Mom so mad at me?" His eyes teared as he looked at Steve.

Steve's shoulders fell, and he took him in his arms. "Oh, Jeffrey." He held him there, pulled him away, and lifted his chin. "Your mother isn't angry at you. She doesn't know what to do with how she feels. She doesn't understand or have any answers, making her feel worse. She'll come around; we must show how much we love and need her. Can you help me do that?"

Jeffrey bravely straightened his shoulders and said, "What can I do to help?"

"Just love her and be here. She needs you, Lori, and Patrick. She needs to know we are here no matter what. That's all we can do."

Steve tenderly touched Jeffrey's shoulder, and Jeffrey fell into a hug again.

"Can Lori and Patrick help, too?"

Steve was then overwhelmed by the love he had for Jeffrey. He was so stalwart and courageous. Taking charge of situations had always been his strength, and here, in this moment, he could see its value more than ever. He watched Jeffrey run off to find his brother and sister and said a silent thanks in his heart for the children he had left, even while the ache in his arms throbbed.

Another week passed, and it was time to return to school. The kids needed to get out and put normalcy back into their lives. Steve was offered more time off but couldn't sit there and watch his wife hurt. He couldn't just do nothing and let the thoughts overtake him.

After much reflection, especially as Maria wasn't speaking yet, he approached Lois.

"Mom, can you help watch the kids and Maria? I've got to work; I need something to do."

Lois hugged her son and held him tenderly. Her gentle arms transferred strength into his own. "Of course, son. I'm here, and we will get through this. I don't know when. I don't know how. But we will get through this, somehow."

They held their embrace for a long time.

Finally, a routine began to come into place.

Get up in the morning. Get Maria into a chair and put lotion on her hands and legs.

Lois would make breakfast and lunches and get the kids up and dressed.

Steve would take the kids to school while Lois took Maria to endless doctor appointments, treatments and then pick up the kids from school at the end of the day.

Day after day ran into the next.

Steve started to become numb. It all blurred, and his emotions were checked into a corner of his mind and locked away. Every day became the same, and Maria continued to sit and stare into the void; he supposed where her heart had gone.

The doctor suggested therapy and medication. Meds were one thing, but she wouldn't even talk to the therapist. They were getting increasingly concerned and had talked to Steve about hospitalization if things didn't improve.

He didn't know when the nightmare would end.

A month or so passed, and Steve came home to find the children in their room coloring pictures. Patrick looked up and said, "Daddy, do you think this will help Mommy know that Allan is okay now?"

Steve took the picture from Patrick and studied it.

It was of two little figures and a larger one with a scribble of green underneath them. The one thing he found truly discernible was that the faces had big smiles.

"Yes, Patrick. This drawing will help. Who is the third person in the picture?"

"It's Grandpa, Daddy!" Patrick said as though it was unnecessary to explain and walked off as if nothing he said was out of the ordinary.

But it touched Steve deeply to see the influence of his mother helping the children know that his brother and sister were with someone to take care of them. He had been trying to wrap his brain around the possibility of nothingness after this life, and it just wouldn't take hold.

Steve's anger at a God led to conversations with this being as if they truly existed in a way he never had before. Sometimes he yelled, sometimes he pleaded, but more and more, he felt that there must be something more. He was even thinking that his children and father might exist somewhere.

His dreams were so vivid and real, reminding him of a place he once knew and longed to be again. His father would smile at him and say words so clearly, "There is a truth."

But he didn't understand or know why. If there was a God and life after death, that was the only truth he needed. What else could there be to know?

His thoughts were interrupted by Lori's soft tug on his pants. "Dad, where is Mommy now?"

"In her chair, honey."

Lori nodded and left the room carrying her picture in her hand.

As always, Maria was sitting in her chair when she felt a small warmth on her arm. She laid her hand on it and felt little fingers. She grasped them and turned herself to face Lori.

Without saying a word, Lori gently climbed up in her mother's lap, stretched her little arms around Maria's neck, and gave a tight squeeze. Then before releasing, she whispered into Maria's ear, "They are okay, Mom. They told me so."

Maria pulled her away quickly and looked at her. Words worked at forming, and finally, she said, "How do you know that? How did they tell you?"

"When I close my eyes, sometimes I see them running and playing with Grandpa or other people. When I go to sleep, they talk to me, too. They're okay, Mommy."

She was so sincere, her voice never wavering. "Mommy, Sarah says she loves you."

Maria pulled her back in and held her tightly. She started crying hard and just kept holding her and rocking. They sat there for an hour, crying, and holding each other.

Finally, Maria got up out of the chair and set Lori down. "Come on, honey, let's go make lunch, shall we?"

Lori smiled at her and handed her the picture. It wasn't of just Sarah and Allan but of Maria, Steve, and the three kids. And above them, clouds with three stick figures on them.

"Can we put this on the fridge, Mommy?"

"We most certainly can, sweetheart. We most certainly can."

That was the turning point for Maria. The words Lori said to her had not come from someone who was on the outside. They weren't the words of her parents saying that they were okay, and she should accept it. They were Sarah and Allan's words. They entered her heart, breaking the ice frozen over it the day she held their lifeless bodies in her arms.

She knew that she would always miss them and that there would be hard days to come, but she also remembered how much she loved them and that they, too, loved her. She could see it, too, when she closed her eyes. The love that came from their eyes when they looked at her told her that. She just hadn't understood it before now. Whatever lay ahead, she knew that didn't die, and her love for them had not died either, and that would carry her through.

That night after they tucked the children into bed, Steve and Maria drove up the hill behind his mother's house. They parked on the ridge overlooking the valley below. City lights glowed above in the haze over the buildings, but being on the hill, they could see the stars in the black sky.

"I'm glad to see you up today," Steve said, hesitating and

almost questioning. He hadn't asked what happened; he only knew that something had for her to be up and about that afternoon. He had been surprised when he came home to find his wife helping to make dinner and talking with the children.

"I'm sorry. I don't know if I can put it into words." Tears were already forming, her voice wavering. She sat there for a few quiet moments and then continued. "I'm not sure what I was supposed to feel after losing them, what I'm still supposed to feel. Everyone kept telling me it was okay, and it wasn't. They told me they were fine, but how could I know? And I was angry that I couldn't just get up and keep going. I couldn't take care of my own family. Others did, and I could only sit there and feel sorry for myself.

"And then I've been having these dreams that have bothered me." She paused momentarily to regain her composure, the emotions still fresh. "But Lori told me today that Sarah and Allan have been talking to her and are okay. But what broke through was what she said next. 'Sarah says she loves you.'"

Tears rolled freely down her cheeks to the crevices of her mouth. "I still hurt so much, but there's a little light now, and I think the dreams are more real, and they are trying to help me. I still want them with me so much, and my arms hurt to hold them. But they are okay."

Steve reached over and took her hand. "I've had dreams, too, and I believe they are okay, too." He paused for a few seconds. "You know how I never believed someone could live after this life?"

She nodded.

"I think I do now. It's the only thing that makes sense."

She put her other hand on his, and they sat silently before heading home. They said all that they needed to say for now.

Chapter Fourteen

STEVE FITFULLY ATTEMPTED SLEEP and, every few moments, rechecked his clock, hoping somehow that time had moved forward enough to justify getting up. During the day each week, he had work, the kids' activities, and the slow improvement of Maria to keep him occupied. At night though, and especially on the weekends, it was much harder to keep moving forward.

Numb was still the default setting, and he tried to keep it that way. But it would catch up with him in the stillness, the unstructured days. Two months now. Two months of missing their two little children's angelic faces, voices, and presence. His heart still ached with the emptiness. He didn't want to burden Maria or his mom, but there was a burning hole inside him that wouldn't stop, and he didn't know how to keep it from taking over.

The dreams didn't help either. They only intensified the burning in Steve's heart.

They seemed to always start with the fire, the blazing red and orange that sent him screaming through smoky darkness, only to find an empty field of ash. Then he would hear his children's laughter, and he would desperately search if only to hold them again.

His father's calm, tender tenor voice followed this, simply repeating, "It's okay. We're here. I'm here."

But Steve couldn't see them. He couldn't touch them or feel them, just empty gray ashes and desperation that smothered him when he opened his eyes.

He slowly got out of bed, trying not to disturb Maria. It was still early, but he didn't know what else to do. He made his way to the bathroom and turned on the shower.

Grief suddenly overwhelmed him, and he crumpled to the cold tile floor. Everything from the last two months cascaded over him and dissipated into the steaming air around him.

His body heaved and shook as undammed tears washed over him as he struggled to breathe.

He found himself pleading, to the universe, "Oh God, if you are there, help me. Help us! I can't do this...." his body heaved through another fit of anguish. He didn't attempt to move or to stop. He just let it take over, allowing the falling water beside him drain away anything left to say.

It was an uneventful day, with chores and playing with children. Everyone was quiet and subdued. Most of the people had stopped coming around as often. But a few remained constant and were becoming friends. In all the years of living in this small community, Steve had never realized how many people he didn't know. His family were never ones to get out much, and they took care of their own, never really getting out to do anything with other people. He was grateful that had not stopped the others from helping his family.

That evening there was an unexpected knock on the door. When Steve opened it, another teacher from the school was there with his son, who Steve recognized as his former student. The surprise on his face showed though he tried to hide it and be gracious.

Mr. Basset's huge frame filled the doorway behind them.

"Mr. Black, how nice to see you. Won't you come in?"

Steve motioned them into the entry, nodding to his son, Ryan. He showed them into the living room and directed them to the loveseat to sit. He was now used to the quiet and reserved Mr. Basset, but he hadn't spent much time with Mr. Black other than faculty meetings and parent conferences.

Maria entered, dabbing her hands on a dishtowel. "Maria, this is Mr. Black and his son Ryan. He teaches with me at the school."

"Good evening. Is there anything I can get for you?" Maria hid her hands in the towel, covering raw skin and scarring.

Mr. Black nervously looked at his hands and shook his head. Ryan chewed his lip, and Mr. Basset sat in his usual silence.

Maria and Steve sat on the couch opposite the men in the chairs and looked at each.

Steve finally broke the silence. "Is there anything we can do for you, Mr. Black? Is everything okay?"

"Oh, no, I, well…. I just…" He sighed. "Okay, here it is. My son and his friends approached me the other day, and I've looked into it, and I think there is something we could do for you. You see, I'm a construction contractor as well as a teacher. Mr. Basset, Greg, is my partner and runs the day-to-day operations while I teach to keep up on the slower months. As you know, I've been teaching shop and architecture for the last couple of years, and we've been looking for a project for some time now." He paused. "I'm sorry, I'm not very good at words. I'm much better with my hands. Here's the short of it. We want to build you a house."

Steve's jaw dropped, and Maria gasped as her hands shot to her face in astonishment. Lois smiled, her eyes crinkling, and her heart swelled.

Steve stammered in protest but was interrupted, this time by Ryan.

"It's okay, Mr. Marksworth. We've worked it all out, and it won't cost you anything. There's a cool program for students to build houses for the community, and usually, it is auctioned off or sold to a family in need. But we've already talked to the program directors, and under the circumstances, they are happy that this will go to someone that we all know and in need."

"It's not that, well, some of it… it's just so much…how?… Why?" Steve couldn't comprehend it all. His thoughts were a jumble of doubts, pride, and gratitude all at the same time.

Maria put her hand gently on his, and her touch reassured and calmed him some.

Greg said, "They will work with you on the plans, and I've already checked into getting the materials donated. Our construction company will provide the additional workforce and expertise, but the boys will mainly run the show. You won't have any expenses, and it will also be a good learning experience for them."

"They really want to do this for you, and I hope you'll say yes," said Mr. Black.

The excitement and anxiety showed in the strained smiles on their faces. Even Mr. Black's neck muscles pulled taught showing the veins. Ryan's eyes were wide with anticipation, and he could barely sit still in his seat. His feet were tapping and legs bouncing, though he tried to keep his hands quietly on his knees.

By now, tears streamed down Maria's face, and she excused herself. Lois followed her out.

Steve had composed himself. He felt a warm and reassuring comfort. He remembered his earlier pleas for help.

With a broken voice, he looked up from his hands and said, "I am touched that you would even consider doing this for us. However, there is one condition before I accept your offer."

Steve tried to put on his most serious teacher face.

A worried frown crossed Ryan's face.

Finally, Steve alleviated the boy's distress. "I get to help!"

Ryan jumped out of his seat.

Mr. Black clapped his hands together and shook them slightly as if in triumph of a long-awaited victory. Greg was calm as if he'd known the outcome all along.

"Well, why don't you call me Doug," said Mr. Black.

"Will do," said Steve.

The men stood and shook hands vigorously. Maria and Lois came back into the room and thanked them. She was smiling, tears still glistening on her cheeks.

When the three left, Steve watched through the glass door pane as Ryan leaped about two feet off the ground, punching his arm into the air.

His father grabbed him around the shoulders, and the two embraced, and Greg clapped Doug on the shoulder.

Steve turned to Maria and gently pulled her into his arms. He whispered in her ear, "My prayer was answered."

She quickly pulled away, looked to Lois, and back again, earnestly searching his eyes, and replied, "You prayed?"

Her confusion was evident. Steve knew she had stopped trying to get him to pray with her a long time ago and, in the process, had stopped herself.

These last couple of weeks, Steve knew Maria had tried. He had heard her, but she could never seem to find the words. Now, here he was doing what she could not. A miracle was happening. Not in what others were doing, but in how Steve grew and changed in ways he had never thought possible.

Lois gently squeezed her son's arm and left them alone.

Maria and Steve went to their room and sat down on the bed. Steve was not typically emotional, and Maria had only seen him teary when the children were born.

Now his raw emotions touched her, and she reached up and caressed his cheek, wiping a tear from the corner of his eye. Then she kissed him and laid her head on his chest. He put his arms around her, burying his face in her hair. The silky softness and lavender scent calmed him.

Chapter Fifteen

$\mathcal{S}$OME DAYS, time drudged slowly by, but other days the hours came and went so quickly that it was difficult for Maria to know what day it was.

The only real structure dictating her life was the still persistent doctor and therapy appointments, with a seemingly endless struggle to make it through each day. It was better, but she doubted whether the pain from this kind of loss ever really became bearable enough.

Lois, too, was starting to finally feel the emotions she had set aside for the last couple of months. Maria was upstairs resting after a hard day of physical therapy. The children were playing, and Steve went over plans with Doug and Basset in the living room.

Lois plucked away cleaning and putting away dishes without any thought or energy. Incredible sorrow had hit her a couple of times late at night when she could hide it all. She had often felt the comforting touch of someone beside her and silently spoke to her husband, "Thank you for watching out for our son."

But today was tough for some reason.

The burning scent of sugar reached her nostrils and awakened her from the trance. "OY!" she exclaimed as she grabbed the hot pads and reached into the oven for the cake she was baking.

Inspecting it, she found just the edges had started to burn. But even so, she started to cry. She sank into a chair and buried her face in the damp, pine-scented dish towel.

A gentle, delicate hand brushed her arm. Startled, she kept her face in the towel to wipe away the blubbering fluids into the rag.

A familiar voice calmed her rushing heart.

"I'm sorry to disrupt you." Mrs. Basset's voice was sturdy and calming. There was something about her that exuded confidence and strength.

It was what Lois needed right now.

Finally, she removed the towel. "I must look like a mess. I'm not sure what came over me just now." Lois apologized.

Mrs. Basset was the guest, and she was taking care of her.

"It's perfectly okay…. I hope to look as good as you in a few years. And you are handling things way better than I ever could." Mrs. Basset's voice reassured Lois, and she looked up to meet her gaze.

"May I sit?"

"Of course, forgive me. Would you like a piece of cake? It's still warm." Lois stood and moved to the cupboards without waiting for an answer, falling into hostess mode.

Mrs. Basset's warm smile reassured Lois as she emphatically replied, "Absolutely! I came over to see if my husband was finished. I should have known better. He may not be chatty normally but get him on construction plans, and we could be here for hours." She chuckled, which put Lois at ease.

Lois cut a piece of cake for each man and took it to them. Then she returned to the kitchen and cut a piece for Mrs. Basset and herself.

After a few moments of silence, Mrs. Basset spoke. "So, how are you all holding up?" Her eyes were steady and didn't shift or cast down like most. She was honest and sincere in her concern. She wanted to know, and Lois was awed by it. Most people had moved on and really didn't want to know the truth, just a polite thing to ask, not necessarily wanting an answer.

Lois looked at this woman who, only a couple of short months ago, was a stranger and now had become a friend.

"We're okay, I think. Some days are harder than others."

She glanced up toward where Maria was resting and listened for the children. "I never expected to deal with anything like this again, especially for little ones. Maria, at least, is starting to heal physically. I know she will never be the same, though. It was hard enough when I lost my husband; I can't even imagine what losing a child would do."

Her eyes reddened now, and she turned back to Mrs. Basset. She choked. "I'm sorry. I don't know what's come over me today."

A warm, tender hand laid on hers, and Lois started to cry again.

"I don't know what to say other than I'm here, and you are not alone." Mrs. Basset's kind words and calm assurance touched Lois, and she cried. Tears burned her cheeks, and her throat tightened as she allowed herself to feel everything that she hadn't had in the few months since the fire, but there was a peace with it that also came over her.

Doug and Greg sat back from the plans while Steve crouched over them, trying to understand what he was looking at. Although he was an English teacher, he had done his fair share of hard work with building and fixing things, especially as a teenager. But he had always been told what to do and never really understood the design end of things. Now, he marveled over the lines and numbers and wondered how all of this meant anything.

Doug chuckled. "Yeah, that's what I looked like the first couple of years of architecture classes, too. But once you figure it out, it makes sense." He looked at Greg and smiled. "It always made sense to you, though, if I remember right."

Greg smiled and replied, "Yeah, it was always my language. I struggled in all of my classes except shop. The math never made sense except when it came to plans and diagrams that I could visualize the end and how it would all come together. It frustrated my teachers to no end. They would say, 'Well, if you can do the math with all of those plans, why can't you do it for class?' But something about the application of it just made it work better in my brain. You'd think story problems would even have helped, but…. if it hadn't been for some good teachers who cared, I wouldn't have made it through school. I am eternally grateful for apprenticeships and tech programs, too."

Doug slapped his hand on Greg's shoulder and nodded. "Yeah, that made me go into teaching instead of fully just into construction. That and the Lord prompting me." He suddenly stopped and turned back to Steve, who had been watching the interchange. "Sorry about that. I forgot not all of us here are religious, which was insensitive of me right now."

Steve was intrigued by his openness about such things with his business partner.

Steve responded, "It's fine. I've never been religious or open about that sort of thing, especially with others. You guys must be pretty close outside of the business to talk about such personal things with each other. I've never had that with anyone except my wife, and we've never really talked about it." He didn't know why he was sharing this. He felt safe and curious about their conversation, and it all spilled out.

Greg and Doug looked at each other, and Greg nodded in approval to whatever passed between them.

Doug looked back to Steve and began to explain. "Well, we're business partners, but it's because of our religious beliefs that this all came to be."

Steve's face contorted into more confusion.

Doug continued. "We've been friends for a very long time. We met and served together while doing service missions for the church we both belong to. We had come from different parts of the country and very different families, but there we were paired up together for a few months, and we just clicked as friends. After we both went home, we stayed in touch.

"Greg went to work and learned with a hands-on apprenticeship route while I went to school. After a few years, we both moved to the same town. We were inspired to start this business together to provide for our families and give back to the Lord in any way we could. It's part of our continued service and written into our business model that we always find a way to help our community and those in need with our talents and ability."

Greg chimed in. "It has not always been easy. Sometimes we've struggled, but we've found that the Lord has always blessed us when we do, and we've been able to be successful over the years because of this, so we keep it going."

Steve sat back in wonder and complete amazement. How could they talk so assuredly about these subjects? It wasn't even something he usually thought about until recently, and now it was ever-present. Still, he didn't know how to find words or feel comfortable even sharing these ideas, let alone openly talking about faith. "Wow, that's actually kind of cool. It's hard for me to talk about my feelings, even on the surface, let alone about something like religion. Yet here you guys are, and you seem so comfortable with it, and well, it's kind of amazing to me."

Greg responded this time. "It wasn't always this easy for me. It is still difficult at times. My family wasn't religious, and when I found the church we both belonged to, I was in high school and did it all on my own. My family understands and accepts me now, but at the time, it wasn't easy at all. I was the only one at my school or in my family. So, it was hard. But when I know something is right, I do it. It wasn't till our mission, that's what we call the service time in our church, that I got better at talking about things. I'm not big on talking anyway, and that pushed me. Lucky for me, Doug here was my training companion, and he was an answer to my prayers that way."

Steve sat processing all of this. He'd never really had any close relationships with other men before. But he saw something here that he wanted; the ability to share and talk about things, to be understood, and to have a brotherhood. That was it; that was the word, brotherhood. His brothers weren't close, and he hadn't realized until this moment that this was something he was missing.

As Mr. and Mrs. Basset left, along with Doug, Steve hoped that one day he could have what they had and share in that way. He had so many questions and thoughts, and that night, as he was next to his sleeping wife, he hoped for something more.

He dozed off with images of his children smiling and dancing in his head.

CHAPTER SIXTEEN

A COUPLE MORE WEEKS PASSED, both monotonous and uneventful. Early one morning, Steve woke up to crying in the next room. He put on his robe and went in to find Patrick on the floor, holding Lori's doll, and sobbing in his sleep.

Gently, he scooped his son up in his arms. He had never realized how small Patrick looked without Allan beside him. It seemed as if there was only half of him there. Patrick opened his eyes and saw his dad.

Patrick dropped the doll when he squeezed his arms around his dad's neck.

Patrick cried through sobs, "I couldn't see his face, Daddy! I couldn't remember what it looked like!" His little body trembled, and Steve could only hold him securely in his arms.

Steve prayed in his heart to know how to help his son, to help his family.

Several minutes later, Patrick was sleeping again. Steve tucked him in bed next to Jeffrey and covered him up.

He returned to his room, but instead of getting back in bed, he knelt on the floor, buried his head in his arms, and poured out his heart.

"Oh God, if you are out there, we need help. Please send us something that will help our family become whole again. Please help us get through this. I don't know what to do anymore." He stopped there, deciding what else to say if there was more. He couldn't think of anything, so he said amen. But he still didn't get up. He knelt there a long time, thinking about his family and what they would do. He did not hear any immediate answers, so he climbed into bed.

He quickly developed a new respect for his mother and all she had gone through. He hoped he could live up to her example, her ability to endure. Again, the burden of everything encompassed his heart and weighed heavy on his mind.

After the children had finally gone to bed and stopped chatting, Maria and Steve sat in the living room, reviewing their bills, the budget, and what they needed. This moved into a discussion of the new house. While there was some excitement, there was also the magnitude of how to afford it.

While they were talking, the doorbell rang.

"Who could that be?" Maria asked.

"I don't know." Puzzled, Steve got up to answer the door.

Maria jumped at Steve's squeal in delight that would rival the children's.

She cautiously entered the foyer. Steve had his arms wrapped tightly around an older man, who was quickly losing his breath beneath the hug.

Maria touched her husband's shoulder. "Steve? I think he might need to breathe, honey."

Steve let go and grasped the man's hand. He then turned to face Maria, glowing like a giddy child.

The man was older, probably midsixties. He was thin, though, and tall. He carried a cane but did not appear frail. His dress was neat, and his manner very pleasant. He, too, was smiling, though not as much as Steve. His face seemed to light up through his soft brown eyes. His gray hair was speckled dark brown or black. He had a broad face, high cheeks, and small lips. But she kept going back to his eyes. There was something there she couldn't explain. They made her feel calm and at peace.

"Maria, this is Mr. Hinckle!" Steve almost shouted it. He was so proud to announce it. "He is the teacher I've told you so much about."

She had long wondered if she would ever meet this man who had meant so much to her husband. Now here he was before her, and she could understand why. There was something about him. Peace, strength; she wasn't sure.

"It's nice to meet you." Maria extended her hand.

He grasped hers with a strong but gentle grip.

"My pleasure," he reassured her. His voice was deep and strong.

"Come in, come in!" Steve was still so excited he almost bound out of the entry to show Mr. Hinckle to the living room.

After they were all seated, Maria asked, "So what brings you here?"

"Well, actually, my wife and I got in last night, and I'm back in town for a while. After speaking with our old friends, we found out about what happened with you and your family. I wanted to make sure Steve and you were okay." There was a concern, genuine, unpitying concern.

Steve looked down at his hands, no longer smiling. "We lost two of our children, Mr. Hinckle. It's been tough. I could have dealt with the house being gone, but losing our children has been hard on us all. We are lost without them. I'm lost. We don't know what to do, and even though things are moving forward, it just feels like I'm drowning some days, you know? I don't know where to turn or what to do."

The words spilled out in a way Maria didn't think possible of her husband.

Maria looked from her husband to Mr. Hinckle. And somewhere in her, she was pleading for help as well. With Steve opening up this way, she knew he must have felt that Mr. Hinckle might have answers of some kind. Her heart jumped at the thought. He had helped Steve once. Could he help them now? Could he help them understand what had happened to their children, to their lives?

Mr. Hinckle didn't look away from either of them. The love and concern softly beamed across and over them. "Steve. Maria. I hope so. There is something I feel I can and should say. I feel in my heart that I must say it, and I hope you will understand it is with all the love I can give. I am here to help you find the truth."

Maria and Steve looked at Mr. Hinckle, and silence lingered.

"What?" Maria was confused and flustered.

How did he know what was bothering them? How could he have known?

She shook her head, trying to understand. Did he say what he just said?

"I said I'm here to help you find the truth." Mr. Hinckle was composed and understanding.

"Why would you say that? How do you know?" asked Steve.

Mr. Hinckle smiled. "Once, a young man lost his father. I tried to share this truth, but my job prohibited me from sharing my beliefs, and my lack of courage didn't help. These last several weeks, as I knew I would be returning here, I hoped that I would be able to see him again."

Steve glanced at Maria, and she knew he was this young man Mr. Hinckle was referring to.

He continued. "Once I heard what happened, though, I wasted no time. I knew I needed to help you find this truth. I have learned over the years not to ignore those promptings, as I once did."

He said it with such surety and power that Maria stared at him. Steve looked down and then back up again. "Mr. Hinckle, I'd like to tell you something I haven't told anyone else until now. From the first night that our children died, I've had these dreams. Sarah, Allan, and even my father tell me to 'find the truth.' I am trying to understand what they mean. God and I are getting on better terms, and I'm starting to believe we will at least exist after this life. Isn't that the truth? What more could there be?"

Maria wrung her hands. "I've had the same dreams." She looked up, her eyes pleading this time. "Please, tell me my children are okay. Tell me what they are trying to say. Please, I need to know."

Steve pulled her to him and held her for a moment. If only he had shared this with her earlier. They could have shared this burden instead of carrying it alone. So much had gone unsaid and unheard in the last month. But no more. They needed each other if they were going to survive this. Steve looked up at Mr. Hinckle, who looked at them both as a father would his child.

Maria pulled herself up as Steve again asked, "Help us, Mr. Hinckle? We need to know."

"My friend, do you remember what I told you after your father died? To think of him as if he was always watching you?"

Steve nodded. "It's what got me through many hard times. You'll never know how much it meant to me. Then, I didn't feel like it was real, but the thought was nice and helped. But now, I'm starting to believe he was somewhere watching me."

Mr. Hinckle nodded. "That is good because Steve, he is. Your children are there with him now. But the truth is not in that alone. There is a larger truth. There is a God. He is our eternal Heavenly Father. He has given us a Plan which allows all families to be together not just for this life but also for the life to come. Not just strangers and people who know each other, but families. Mothers. Fathers. Daughters. Sons. Families united and bonded together for eternity. Know that your family lives beyond this life. I know that your children are whole and well and that you will one day be reunited. There is truth in this, and I want to help you and Maria find this truth and come to know it for yourselves."

He spoke with power, and the words were hot and piercing the center of their hearts.

How could he be so certain? Could it be that there was such a plan, and that she would see her children again, not just as some vague acquaintances as she had been taught, but actually, as her children whom she had held and loved for so long? And with that thought, something moved within her, and she felt the words, "Yes, Mommy, it's true!"

Steve, too, was letting these words sink in. It was so new. These thoughts had never occurred to him before. And even though they were new, they made sense. Not to his mind, which was spilling over with questions and doubt, but in his heart, there was peace. Somehow, he knew what this man was telling him was the truth. Could there be that certainty in life? To know that your family would be together no matter what happens in this life? Oh, if only it could be!

Mr. Hinckle was quiet. He was letting the young parents process what he had just told them. "There is so much I could tell you, but I think this is enough for now. I will say this, though, there is a religion, church, which teaches this plan. It is the only one on earth that teaches this, and which has the power and authority from God to do such things. I belong to this church and would like to send some friends around to help teach you more about it if that is okay?"

They looked at each other and back at him. They both nodded, then Steve asked, "Will you be here? Can we count on you to continue to help us?"

"Always, Steve. I've made plans to be here for some time. I'll help wherever I can. But for now, I'd better head back, or the Mrs. will be getting worried. One day back in town, and I don't think she was expecting me to be off and going already."

Mr. Hinckle stood, looking a bit weaker than when he'd come. It was as if something was taken out of him. Steve saw him to the door, and when Steve returned, he and Maria stared at each other.

Maria noticed a seriousness in Steve's eyes that she had never seen before. But there was something else, too. Could it be hope?

"Can it be true?" Maria asked.

"I don't know. I hope so. Wouldn't it be wonderful if it was? My mind argues with the concept, all my logic. But the feeling I had when Mr. Hinkle spoke was incredible. If what he says is true, our children are ours, Maria. They are still ours!"

He pulled her to him and said again, "They are still ours!"

They held each other for a long time. Then together they started a new tradition. That night they prayed together, as husband and wife, and thanked God for sending them Mr. Hinckle, their family, and answers to their prayers.

CHAPTER SEVENTEEN

*H*IS WORN SHOES contrasted with the new floors and pristine foyer. Leaning over with elbows on his knees and face in his hands, the somber young man in a clean but aged suit impatiently tapped his foot.

Wise beyond his years. Elder Harris' mind raced.

Why does the new president need to see me right now?

He waited like a middle school student outside the principal's office, everything running through his head of what he could possibly have done wrong this time. It didn't make sense either since he worked in the mission office, and he and his companion had long given up going anywhere but on errands for the president.

The door swung open, and a young new Elder left the president's office and sat across the entranceway. The new Elder looked shell-shocked, and Elder Harris smirked a little, wondering if he had also looked that young and scared when he arrived.

Responding to the still open door and a wave of a hand, he wanted to see what was next.

The new mission president sat behind the desk, his back now to Elder Harris; he stared out the window.

Elder Harris knew not to interrupt him, so he waited patiently for the president to address him.

A few more minutes waiting for the president wouldn't hurt him.

The president turned and faced the young man. "Have a seat, Elder Harris. Tell me about your sister."

Elder Harris sat down but was shocked at what the president asked.

What? How did he know? And why now?

That was not something he talked about openly, even with his companions, and very few knew he even had a sister.

He gulped then asked, "What would you like to know, president?"

"Tell me about your sister," he simply restated.

Elder Harris hadn't talked about her much in years, but he thought about her every day. She was the reason he was here on this mission. She was the reason he was probably still alive. "It's a long story, president."

"I cleared my schedule for the rest of the afternoon. We have time."

More uncomfortable now, Elder Harris drew a breath in and thought back to white hospital hallways and a smile that never ended. After sharing the story, he breathed deeply and looked back up at the older man.

The president looked deeply into Elder Harris' eyes and said, "You are going to be transferred one last time, and there is a special family who needs you now more than you know."

Perplexed and surprised, Elder Harris simply returned the gaze and said, "Wherever the Lord needs me, President Hinckle."

The new Elder White and Elder Harris were walking down the street toward the Marksworth's family residence.

Only out of the Missionary Training Center for about one week, White looked like he was sixteen years old with light blond hair, a skinny frame, and glasses.

Elder Harris found him a little "nerdy."

Elder Harris, on the other hand, was only a few months from going home, and the exhaustion and exhilaration of the last twenty-two months was starting to show. He was taller, broadly built, and had a permanent tan on his face. His clothes were not gleaming or as neat as they used to be. But his eyes shone with a wisdom one only gains through experience. Together, they looked like an odd pair.

"Elder Harris?" White still seemed anxious to address his companion and was unfamiliar with his surroundings and situation.

"Yes, Elder?" Harris's voice resonated in a deep baritone.

"Have you ever tracked here before?" White's voice still almost cracked like he was still starting puberty.

Harris couldn't tell if it was from nerves or the fact that he was really that young. He thought back to his first in-the-field week as a missionary. Had he sounded that naïve? Had he really ever looked that young and insecure? It gave him patience and understanding of his new companion to think that he, too, had been where he stood now.

"Yes, I have. A couple of times." This was his second area and the second time he had served in this part of the mission. He had thought it strange to be assigned to the exact same area but didn't question it. He thought back to the last time he had walked down this street.

He began to tell the story. "We had taken a wrong turn with my senior companion. We decided to track down this street out of pure desperation to find out where we were and how to find our dinner appointment. It is the very house we are going to tonight that we found sympathy. Every house we stopped at had no answer, or the occupants peeked out, saw who we were, and didn't open the door."

Harris chuckled. "One woman threatened to call the cops on us if we ever came back. I don't know why people think that way, but I still find it amusing."

He was silent for a moment and then continued. "Anyway, we came to this house, an older lady answered. I don't think she'd ever met any missionaries before because she actually asked what we were doing. So, we went on to explain who we were and if she was interested. She was very kind and indicated that she wasn't interested in any religion right then, but if we needed a drink of water, we were more than welcome to come in and cool off a bit. So, we took her up on her offer for the drink, of course, and also informed her of our situation. She was very gracious and allowed us to use her phone to call the family to come and get us. We talked a little while we waited, then we thanked her, and we went on our way. Come to think of it, I hadn't thought of her again until now. I wonder if she still lives there?"

Harris noticed a young boy sitting on the steps as they drew closer to the house. He seemed about eight or nine years old. But instead of playing or running around like the other boys his age, he was just sitting there looking up into the sky.

"Hello, young man." Harris used his best big brother voice. He remembered how he liked to be talked to by his older brothers. He had particularly liked it when they made him sound more grown up.

Startled from his thought, Jeffrey turned toward the tall Elder. His eyes darted between them, sizing them up, and stared at them curiously. "Hello."

Elder White spoke up now. "Can you tell us if this is the Marksworth's house?"

"Yeah," he answered, still staring at them.

Elder White seemed confused at why Jeffrey was staring at them and wasn't being more helpful. "Well, are they home?"

"Elder," Harris chided under his breath. Then in a more friendly and understanding manner, Harris squatted down next to Jeffrey.

"So, what were you looking at up there?"

Jeffrey seemed to relax as he looked into Harris' eyes.

"I was trying to see if I could see heaven." He was very matter of fact and held no hesitation in saying it. There was no hint of a joke in it, and that caught Harris by surprise.

"Really. Why do you want to see heaven?" He had learned to take advantage of any opportunity, no matter how small or out of place it might be.

Now Jeffrey seemed shy and reserved. He looked down at the cement and heaved a sigh.

Harris put his hand on the boy's shoulder. "It's okay. You don't have to tell me." He waited a minute until Jeffrey looked up again. His eyes were red with small stains where tears had started to roll down his cheeks. Harris decided to change the subject and avoid the embarrassment.

"So, what's your name?" he asked gently; all the while, White was standing back watching.

"Jeffrey." He perked up a little and smiled.

"I'm Elder Harris, and this is Elder White." He took his hand from Jeffrey's shoulder and extended his hand to him.

They shook, and Elder White took his turn as well. "Are your parents at home?"

"Yeah. Come on in." Jeffrey stood, wiped his face a little, and led them into the house.

Something was familiar when Lois greeted the Elders from the kitchen. It was a strange name, especially considering how young they were. One of them, though, she recognized and couldn't place how or where.

Steve came bounding in, chasing after Lori, who squealed as he grabbed her up. When he saw that there were new people in the room, he sheepishly cuddled Lori to his chest while she shyly hid her face. "Sorry! I just found out you arrived."

"It's okay," Elder Harris replied. It reminded him of home. He stretched out his hand, shook Steve's, and then turned to Lois. "We've met before, though you probably don't remember it. We were thirsty, and you gave my other companion and me a drink. We needed a phone as we were lost, and you gave us directions and a phone."

Lois smiled with the reference.

"Ah, yes! I thought you looked familiar. It's been a while now, and I didn't see you around again. I'm assuming it went well that day?"

"Well, we made it home safe and sound with dinner, so I'd call it a success."

It was easy with her. She reminded Steve of his mother, and

that helped. Elder Harris motioned to his companion. "This is Elder White, new to our lovely part of the world."

"Welcome, Elder White," Lois said, smiling at his awkwardness as he put out his hand to shake hers.

"Yes, welcome," said Steve as he shook Elder Harris' hand. "Won't you come in and take a seat? Maria! The Elders are here!"

While they all took seats in the living room, Maria sat on the bed in their bedroom. It had been a couple of weeks since Steve's old teacher, Mr. Hinckle, had visited them. She had since grown worried that it had all been in her head. That what she felt that night was just hopeful wishes of grief. She was afraid that it would all dissipate and not be real, and she didn't want to spiral again. She was concerned about what they would want to know and the judgment of others in seeing her there like she was, still recovering.

Her hands were now in light gauze wrappings with stretch gloves meant to help ease the healing and keep the scarring away. Mobility was limited, and she wondered what they would think. Still walking slowly, she made her way down the stairs and to the living room. She rounded the corner and saw two very young boys, one who reminded her of Allan if he had lived to grow up. It struck her and made her stop and hesitate. How on earth could these young people teach them anything? How could they even know anything about life, let alone God and His plan?

A knock at the door interrupted her thoughts, and she took advantage of the distraction to answer the door.

Mr. Hinckle was there with his wife at his side.

"Come in. It's a pleasure to see you again." Maria turned to the woman. "You must be Mrs. Hinckle?"

The wrinkled, kind face smiled back and gently took the gloved hands in hers so as not to put any pressure. "Marjorie, please." Her gentleness surprised Maria and put her at ease. She welcomed them into the other room, where everyone was now getting situated.

Steve stood and walked over to the open arms of Mr. Hinckle and hugged him. He shook Marjorie's hands and greeted them, motioning to take seats in the formed close circle.

The Elders stood and shook hands as they walked by. "president," Steve heard one of them say.

Huh, I wonder why they called him that?

For a moment, they all just sat, not knowing how or where to begin. Steve finally broke the awkward silence with his now-pressing question. Looking around, he cleared his throat and then asked, "Mr. Hinckle, why did they just call you president?"

President Hinckle chuckled a little. "Yes, well, you can be assured that I haven't run or been elected to office or anything like that. In our faith, we have missions around the world, where young people, and old, like the Elders here, go and serve communities and share messages of hope. They have individuals and couples that they ask to be presidents over these missions to help with organization and guidance. So mostly, I'm just a glorified organizer and travel guide in a lot of ways. My wife here is really the one who keeps everything going and everyone on track." Marjorie smiled at the compliment and lightly shook her head.

Lois now chimed in with her query. "Why are you called Elders? You aren't very old."

This time Elder Harris smiled and responded.

"I don't know how much you know the Bible, but in the organization of the church in the old days, teachers and those who were asked to serve and work within the church were often called Elders. We are given the title, office, and authority of Elders for our mission as we go and serve and teach. When we go back home, we go by our given names again."

Maria, curious now, asked, "So how long do you serve? How old are you?"

Elder White responded, "Well, I'm nineteen, and we usually are called for around two years for boys. When a girl goes on a mission, it's around eighteen months."

Jeffrey asked, "But why would you go out and do that? Do they pay you? Do you get famous?"

"No," said Elder Harris. "We go because Heavenly Father asks us to and because we love Him and want to help Him show how much He loves everyone. We go and serve others. In fact, there was a king, a very long time ago, who lived on this continent before it was our country. And he told his people that whoever is in the service of his fellow beings is only in the service of his God. Pretty cool, huh?"

Elder White chimed in, feeling more at ease and confident. "We don't do it to get famous and pay our own way. So, really, we do want to help others."

Jeffrey raised his eyebrows, not sure if he could believe that anyone would want to pay to go out and work. But Steve, Lois, and Maria all gazed at these people. There was a familiar aurora about them, and as they talked about serving others, they reflected back on all the people who had come and helped in the first days following the fire.

Maria thought back to the students offering to build a house for them and all that had transpired. These people had come in without asking anything in return, freely given their time, goods, and love. Many of them had continued to come and visit over the last while, bringing children to play with, occasional treats, and friendship.

Yes, there was truth in what they said; how young men knew and understood this at their age was beyond her.

President Hinckle spoke up now. "With that, the Elders always like to share a special message with you and then answer any questions you might have, too. Tonight though, I want Elder Harris to share his story."

President Hinkle turned to Elder Harris with a smile and nodded. Elder Harris took a deep breath in and composed himself. He knew it was coming. He had prepared for it since meeting the president. It was still hard, though. He started his story:

"Well, I grew up in a small town in Utah my whole life. People there were, well, let's say, not as generous with God's grace. I was bullied for being a little different, and it's hard to go to church and sit with all of those kids, knowing what they say and do in the play yard and then try to talk about forgiveness, love, and them acting holy. My sister got it worse, though. She was born with Down's syndrome, and so she not only looked different, which they didn't understand, she was slower intellectually, too. They were cruel to her, even when they knew how sick she got. But wow! That girl would just love them and forgive them and still try to be their friend. Mom said it was Down's Syndrome that she didn't understand. I didn't think much of it then, but now, I think there was definitely more to it than that. Her body may have been imperfect, but her spirit was beyond perfect in every way. I always wondered why God would allow such a wonderful soul to come to earth and be treated that way. But I wasn't much better than the other kids, either, some days.

"Anyway, when I became a teenager, I rebelled against everything—parents, school, church, and God. I saw the hypocrisy at church, my sister, and my life, and I couldn't believe everything everyone said. With that, I also got in with the wrong crowd. I spiraled and got mean, especially to Natalie. She tried to follow me everywhere. She wanted to do everything with me. I'd yell at her, tell her I didn't want her around, and well, I'm ashamed to say, I wasn't the best brother at all. But every day, she would ask. Every day her face would light up when she saw me. Every day she wanted to follow me and be with me.

"Natalie was just so patient and so loving, and I'd come home really late, drunk, and angry, and she knew and would hear me. My parents didn't want to see me like that, and I knew that they were ashamed, or so I thought anyway. But Nat would wake up and come into my room and give me a hug and say she loved me. She didn't care about anything or anyone; she just loved me, even when I couldn't love myself.

"Then, one day, my mom called me while I was out doing who knows what. I didn't answer the phone, but she left me a message. 'Your sister is in the hospital. Come.'

"Nat's heart had always been an issue. I learned to hate hospitals as they meant I was left wandering the halls while my parents took turns being by her when the other wasn't working. They knew that even the thought of them made me sick, so once I was old enough to be alone, they stopped making me come. But this time, her tone was different, and she said to come, so I went. I was a mess—my clothes, my hair, everything, and especially my attitude.

"But when I walked into that room and saw her there with all her cords and tubes, it crushed me.

"She was asleep, and Mom's face was tired and helpless. Dad just stared at her, me, and then back to her. We knew that this day could come, but Mom said, 'Not much longer,' and I broke.

"We sat vigil by her bed.

"Mom and Dad stepped out to talk to the doctor one night about what was next, arrangements, etc. I just sat there next to her, holding her little hand, and wishing I had been better, and cursing myself for the horrible person I had been, especially to her. I felt a squeeze of my hand and looked up. Nat's eyes were open, and she smiled at me like she did, and I cried. 'Don't cry,' she told me. 'It's okay.'

"No! It's not! I'm the one who isn't worthy to be here. You deserve life so much more than I do. Why is God doing this to you? To us?

"I gushed out all of my thoughts and feelings, not thinking she would understand. But, for a moment, it was as if there were no limitations, and she was a grown woman speaking to me. 'Jon, it's okay. I will be okay, and we will see each other again.'

"I looked at her, speechless.

"Then she said, 'You're going to be okay, too.'

"I scoffed. Yeah, me, the screw-up and prodigal son.

"She grabbed my hand as if she knew what I was thinking and said, 'I love you! Heavenly Father loves you! You are going to be okay!'

"That was it. She closed her eyes and fell asleep. She never woke up again. The next morning, she slipped away, and my parents went on and on about God's plan. But I didn't know. I didn't have their certainty in anything, let alone a God who would leave me here and take the sweetest soul away. But Nat's last words just kept eating at me, and every time I went to do something, it was as if they were reminding me and calling me back to where I belonged.

"It was a long road back. I fought it the whole way. But, eventually, I did let that love back in, and I was determined to show that love the way Natalie would have wanted. That is why I am out here on a mission, hoping to help others how my sister helped me."

The room was silent for several minutes.

A palpable spirit of love and peace filled in and around everything.

Mr. Hinckle nodded and finally broke the silence. "The other night when I visited, I told you that your children are in heaven. That they are with God, and you will see them again. Tonight, I want to add something else, and then the Elders here can share why and how what I'm saying is possible and let you ask any questions you want. Not only are we able to see our families again after we die, but my friends, you will still be a family. Families are not just temporary, but an eternal organization that our Heavenly Father has gifted us if we choose them."

A warmth now filled the air and pressed in on them. President Hinckle then stated, with confidence and power Maria had never experienced before.

"I know that our Heavenly Father loves each and every one of us, His children. He knows us and our pain and longings. He has a plan of Happiness that allows for us all to return to Him and continue on together, never to be separated ever again. Families are the central core of this plan and who we are and can be. Heavenly Father knows and loves each of you!"

While Mr. Hinckle did not raise his voice, almost no more than a strong whisper at times, his words penetrated the empty corners in their hearts.

No one spoke or moved for a very long time until Lori and Patrick shifted a little, and Maria noticed they were restless for having already exceeded their sit-still time.

At that, Elder Harris looked at each of them in the eyes, not speaking but taking his time. In the end, he ended his gaze on Jeffrey, who sat solemn and still. Catching his gaze, he said, "I also know this to be true. I know that I will be with my sister again. Heavenly Father sent His son, Jesus Christ, to make it possible. I know His plan of Happiness is for all of us if we accept it."

Jeffrey nodded, and Elder Harris then looked to Patrick and Lori until each of them returned a nod as well.

Throughout the remainder of the evening, the Elders taught the family about the restoration of their religion and a special book of scripture that they gave them copies of. They laughed, they pondered, and they felt something new but real and never wanted it to end.

CHAPTER EIGHTEEN

*M*ARIA HADN'T PERSONALLY PRAYED in a very long time, at least formally and definitely not out loud. It was quiet in the house. Too quiet. She suddenly felt extreme loneliness and emptiness with the kids at school and Lois out on an errand.

Usually, she would have Sarah with her. This time of day would be a quick snack with her meds and cuddle story time. She could still feel that small form and warmth snuggled in with Sarah's head on her chest, pointing at the pictures, and trying to say the simple sounds that animals would make in a story or the repeated phrases of a nursery rhyme.

Within seconds, her body heaved with grief. This happened a lot still, especially when she was alone. When it started, and others were around, she would push it down, tuck it away, and hope it wouldn't show. She didn't want them to worry about her, and she didn't want to go back to the place she was at the beginning.

But, when she was alone, she let it come and take over for a while.

Maria crumpled to the floor. She clutched the little doll the kind woman had given to Lori. She squeezed it, hoping that it would bring some small semblance of the life she had lost.

She cried out, "God, please! I can't do this anymore. How can I go on without them? You say they are okay, but they aren't here with me! I needed them! Why?! PLEASE!!!"

The words poured out of her amid the tears pouring down her cheeks, and she didn't attempt to stop either.

Curled in a heap on the floor, she lay there for what seemed like hours.

Finally, the storm calmed down, but she didn't feel any energy to move. She just wanted to stay, lay there, numb, and thoughtless.

A light knock echoed through the house. She didn't move.

After a moment, another tapping.

She pulled herself up and, with effort, started to the door.

Maria wiped her eyes and straightened herself out a bit, sniffling on her way to the door. When she opened it, she froze and clutched the doll closer.

A familiar woman stood on the porch.

Her eyes went to the doll, then back up to Maria's face, biting her lip and wringing her hands.

"Hi... I'm Holly. I came over a while ago to bring some things for the kids with the Bassets; I don't know if you remember me."

Maria knew the Bassets well by now. Mrs. Basset came by frequently to check on them and talk for a while. She found it kind and great, but she had yet to connect with her.

"Yes, I remember you. You gave this doll to our Lori. She loves it so much, thank you!" Maria noticed that Holly looked

at the doll again, chewed her lip, and looked down before looking back at Maria.

Holly clasped her hands even more tightly. "I'm glad she's
enjoying her. I wanted to check on you, though. I'm sorry if I
interrupted anything."

Maria realized that she must look quite a mess at this point.
Her shabby baggy clothes, red tear-stained eyes, no makeup,
and still bandaged hands probably made her look like she wasn't
doing well. Which, honestly, at this moment, was the truth.
While normally she would say she was fine and cordially excuse
herself, something this time was different, and tears started back
down her cheeks. Immediately, Holly was through the doorway,
put her arms around Maria, and held her.

Maria sat at the table, and Holly brought her chamomile
tea. There didn't seem to be any need for words. Somehow, they
knew each other's hearts.

After a while, Maria looked at Holly and asked, "So, how are
you?" laughing a little, and Holly smiled, too.

"Oh, I'm hanging in there." While not bitter, the tone and
smile changed as Holly's eyes again made their way to the doll
that now lay on the table.

Maria noticed and asked, "Was this doll special to you or
your daughter?"

It felt good to get out of her own thoughts for a minute, and
it seemed like Holly needed to talk, too.

"Sort of." Holly's eyes stayed on the doll, and she bit her lip
again.

Maria didn't push; she just sat and waited.

After several minutes, Holly looked at Maria, pursed her lips
to keep her composure, and then spoke. "Our first baby was

stillborn. A little girl. This was the doll we had bought for her to come home from the hospital to when we first found out."

"Oh, my heavens! I didn't know. I'm so sorry." Maria wondered if she should offer the doll back. That must have been so hard for her to give away.

"It's okay, and it's okay for Lori to have the doll."

Maria wondered how she had somehow known but just kept listening.

"It's been a few years now, and even though I know she's waiting for us in heaven, it's hard, and there are days I just don't deal as well as I would like, you know?"

Maria did know.

"I was starting to feel that this morning, so I went on a walk to try and clear my head before the kids got home from school, and somehow, I ended up here. I realized that maybe you needed someone, and now I needed you."

Maria simply nodded; a shared understanding again passed between them as they sipped the tea.

"Do you mind if I ask if they know what happened?"

"I don't mind. It's just hard to share sometimes." Holly took a deep breath and composed herself. "It had been a hard pregnancy from the beginning. Jason and I were married only a few months, and he worked a lot. In the last month, I didn't feel right. I'd already had Braxton Hicks for a couple of months, but something changed, and I always thought something was wrong. I went in at least a couple times a week, and while the doctor was kind, he would hear the heartbeat and say everything was fine. She wasn't moving much, and they just said she was out of room and not to worry. So, I kept pushing the feelings away, chalked it up to the first time and being overly paranoid."

She paused, breathed deeply in and out. "At the last appointment, they couldn't find the heartbeat. They did an ultrasound, and still nothing. She was gone, and they didn't know for how long. I was alone, so I had to call Jason, and he rushed over."

Another pause. "The worst part is that they have you deliver the baby, and there you are hearing babies cry, expecting a warm little body on top of yours, and instead, there is just nothing."

She must have noticed Maria's horrified face because she added, "Oh, they did let me hold her. It was actually a special moment. Jason and I both felt her spirit there with us, and they let us hold her until we were ready, but…."

Maria thought back to the hospital room holding her own children for the last time. Her heart ached not only for herself, but for Holly as well.

Holly stopped, unable to go on.

Maria knew. She couldn't have imagined going through labor and birth only to hand them over before ever knowing them. But she knew what it was like to hold that precious little silent body and never let it go.

Holly smiled again as she put her cup down. "On my mission in England, their answer to everything seemed like a good cup of tea. I always felt bad turning them down since we don't drink tea unless it's herbal. I've taken to drinking herbals to help with things, and I can understand a little now why. Something about it warms you up from the inside out."

Maria didn't fully understand the reference but just nodded. Sometimes something warm and sweet just did something to calm her, too.

"So, you served a mission? Are you also a Mormon?" Maria wasn't sure if asking was polite, but she was curious.

"Ah, yes. I am a member of the Church of Jesus Christ of Latter Day Saints, as they want us to say, but I still kind of like our nickname of 'Mormons,' too. And yes, I served a mission in England. That seems like forever ago."

"What made you want to go there?" Maria was now invested in knowing why these young people would go and leave their families for so long.

"Well, I didn't choose where I went, just to go. I was in college, just going along and doing my degree like everyone else, but I didn't feel it, you know? It just wasn't where I felt like I was supposed to be. So, I talked to our church leaders and my family, and I thought maybe a mission would help me figure out what I should do instead. I'd never felt like I had to go on one, like others around me. But why not, I thought. I didn't get a bad feeling about it, so. Anyway, when young people, or older people, too, want to serve a mission, they fill out paperwork. That, and a recommendation from their local leader, gets submitted to the prophet and apostles, overall leaders of our faith, and they pray about it and give us callings where they feel the Lord wants us to be."

Maria's face must have shown a very perplexed look.

Holly chuckled. "Yeah, a lot of people in England gave me that same look. I know it seems strange and completely abnormal for kids barely out of high school, who would normally be out planning their lives, partying, etc., to give it all up to pay to go out to some place they don't even choose to talk to people they don't even know, about something those people don't even want to hear about. But, you know, I grew so much and learned more about myself and who I wanted to be. Yes, I went out to serve others and share and teach others about what I felt was true, but in the end, I really discovered who I was as a child of God, my place and purpose, and how I wanted to live my life to return to Him one day, and that has guided everything since. I didn't realize then how much I would need that until we lost our little girl. Don't get me wrong. I know we will be a forever family, and that she is still mine and everything, but that doesn't help a lot when you are sitting alone with empty arms, and everyone knows and looks at you. God and I have had some very frank conversations, and well, I'm still not always happy with Him about it. But I do trust Him and know He knows more than I do, so I keep going."

"That sounds amazing. There are so many times when I've been raising my kids that I felt like I didn't know who I was outside of them or the everyday things we had going on. They've been my whole world and identity for so long, and now…" Maria's voice trailed off.

Holly softly placed her hand over Maria's.

Maria hardly felt her touch, but the warmth was there, nonetheless.

"I know." That's all she could say.

They sat there for a while again, and then Holly glanced at her watch.

"Wow! Um, I've got to get home before the kids do. If you'd like, we can get together again and talk, or not talk, or do things if you want. I found that, even though I just wanted to be alone, it was harder, and I wished some days that I had someone to go out with or just be there. We don't have to, but if you need, just let me know, okay?"

She wrote her number down on the fridge post board. Maria noticed she was biting her lip again and that her other hand tightened.

"I'd like that, I think," Maria said. She'd not had any friends since college days, and with the kids, especially Sarah, she didn't have time or a place to really make any since then. It felt good to just talk to someone who understood and had been through something similar. Already, she didn't feel so alone anymore.

Holly's smile was genuine, and the hands calmed to her sides. She watched Holly walk away before shutting the door.

Maria felt lighter and more hopeful than she had in a long time.

Chapter Nineteen

ESTLESS, Maria slipped out of bed and stepped out into the hallway, careful not to wake Steve. Her legs were working better now, but the scars limited movement, likely permanently.

Stepping as lightly as possible, she went to the door of Lori's room. Pressing gently, she gazed at the sleeping figure, listening for her breathing like she did when she was a baby.

Lying there, with her pink light flushed cheeks, Lori appeared smaller than she really was.

Maria moved on to the boys' room. A soft glow met her as the door cracked. Jeffrey had his book light out and was engrossed in a text. She smiled and prepped herself to appear upset at his violation of curfew hours. Then she noticed the book in his hands.

Soft blue cover with gold embossed writing. It was the book the missionaries had given each of them. Maria had yet to start it; she wanted to do it with Steve, but here was her son reading it through the night.

Jeffrey noticed her and gave her his usual guilty smile while at the same time glowing with excitement. His eyes reflected wonder and joy.

Maria envied him and wondered what he had just read to bring this on. She nodded to him, winked, and blew him a kiss.

He turned out the flashlight and carefully placed the book on the side table.

Turning back, she looked at her own bedroom door, then at the stairs. Instead, she went down to the kitchen.

A copy of the book lay on the table. She sat in a chair, picked it up, and held it for several seconds.

She opened it to where the missionaries had marked it as the words seeped in of the resurrected Christ on the American continent, a familiar warmth filled in the cracks. The same warmth and light she had felt lying in the hospital bed, seemingly unconscious.

Hungrily, she poured over each chapter until she hit a section that made her stop and reread it over and over again. Maria's heart swelled, and new tears brimmed at the corners of her eyes, not out of pain or sorrow but a healing hope.

Steve rolled over and felt the emptiness in the bed beside him.

He forced himself awake and looked around the room to find nothing.

A slight lurch in his stomach forced him to sit up. "Maria?"

He called out softly, and when no reply came, he searched for her.

Once in the hallway, he noticed the light from the kitchen and went down. He stopped abruptly at what he saw.

Maria, reading with the light reflecting the wet lines down her cheeks. The calmness he felt in the room and around her was palpable.

Gently, he walked over, laid his hands on her shoulders, and leaned his head in close to her, pressing lightly. The smell of strawberry lavender engulfed him.

Maria leaned back. She pressed her cheek to his, then turned to him, and their eyes met.

Tears poured down her face and dripped off her chin, but she was smiling.

Without speaking, she looked back at the page, found the verses with her finger, and directed him to them.

He sat down next to her and took the book.

He read out loud.

"And it came to pass that he commanded that their little children should be brought.

So they brought their little children and set them down upon the ground round about him, and Jesus stood in the midst, and the multitude gave way till they had all been brought unto him.

And it came to pass that when they had all been brought, and Jesus stood in the midst, he commanded the multitude that they should kneel down upon the ground.

And it came to pass that when they had knelt upon the ground, Jesus groaned within himself and said: Father, I am troubled because of the wickedness of the people of the house of Israel.

And when he had said these words, he himself also knelt upon the earth; and behold he prayed unto the Father, and the things which he prayed cannot be written, and the multitude did bear record who heard him.

And after this manner do they bear record: The eye hath never seen, neither hath the ear heard, before, so great and marvelous things as we saw and heard Jesus speak unto the Father;

And no tongue can speak, neither can there be written by any man, neither can the hearts of men conceive such great and marvelous things as we both saw and heard Jesus speak, and no one can conceive of the joy which filled our souls at the time we heard him pray for us unto the Father.

And it came to pass that when Jesus had made an end of praying unto the Father, he arose; but so great was the joy of the multitude that they were overcome.

And it came to pass that Jesus spake unto them and bade them arise.

And they arose from the earth, and he said unto them: Blessed are ye because of your faith. And now behold, my joy is full.

And when he had said these words, he wept, and the multitude bare record of it, and he took their little children, one by one, and blessed them, and prayed unto the Father for them.

And when he had done this, he wept again;

And he spake unto the multitude, and said unto them: Behold your little ones.

And as they looked to behold they cast their eyes towards Heaven, and they saw the heavens open, and they saw angels descending out of Heaven as it were in the midst of the fire, and they came down and encircled those little ones about, and they were encircled about with fire, and the angels did minister unto them."

(Book of Mormon 3 Nephi Chapter 17 verses 11–24)

He didn't fully understand what he had read, yet somehow, there was a power in his feelings.

He visualized the words and saw his children there with a man, the Christ, and the glow of a fire surrounding them as well. Then he reread again, the lurch of his heart choked into his throat, and he caught his breath.

Looking into Maria's eyes, they held hands, pondering their feelings, and wondering at the new truth they felt in their hearts.

CHAPTER TWENTY

*S*UNSHINE FLOWED IN BROKEN RAYS as Maria hesitantly stepped through to the foyer. Comforted by the gentle pressure of the back of Steve's hand and Jeffrey at her side, she allowed herself to breathe. She clutched her hands nervously, remembering a few days earlier invitation.

The Elders had returned for a meal and a message, along with President Hinckle. While talking, Steve and Maria shared their experience from the past evening while reading the Book of Mormon.

"Sister Marksworth." Elder Harris' kind and gentle voice had followed a period of silence as they had all reflected on their discussion.

"Maria, please." She felt she constantly reminded him and didn't quite understand the term or the formality.

Elder White nervously looked between them, but Elder Harris merely continued. "Sorry, yes, Maria. What you are describing is what we call the Holy Ghost or spirit. That peace and warmth is one way in which Heavenly Father confirms what is true to us. We know it's been difficult for you, and that it can still be a struggle to get out at times. However, we wondered if you'd like to join us at church on Sunday. They do have soft seats, and we'll do all we can to make sure you are comfortable. But, after hearing your experience, we feel that you would possibly feel more of the Holy Spirit."

Maria's eyes found Steve's, and his face was anxious for her. She had been more self-conscious lately, especially of her painful and scarred hands. Even going to physical therapy was a trial she endured.

Lois said, "I would love to go and help with the children as well. I'm interested in what to expect."

The reprieve for a moment allowed Maria a chance to figure out what she could say.

Elder White elaborated. "We have what we call Sacrament meeting. During this meeting, we pray, sing hymns, and listen to other members discuss their experiences, faith, and gospel topics. We also partake of the sacrament, bread and water that has been blessed, in remembrance of Jesus Christ, what he did for us, and our personal baptismal covenants."

Sitting on the floor next to the Elder, Patrick squinched his face. "That doesn't sound very fun."

They all chuckled, but Jeffrey chided him, "It's not supposed to be 'fun,' Patrick. It's supposed to be where we learn about church. Duh!"

Lori, usually pretty quiet during these conversations, cuddled her doll and asked, "It sounds nice. Can I bring my doll?"

President Hinckle had attended every one of their discussions. He smiled gently at all the children and replied, "Yes, Jeffrey, you are correct. But that doesn't mean it's all boring, at least I hope not. The speakers often try to make it interesting if they can, but I know many families bring some things to help, like coloring, etc. I'm sure we can find some things for you, Patrick. Also, there is another meeting in the second hour, where children go to. It's called Primary, and they sing, have activities, and have a little more fun classes while their parents go to their own class."

He turned his tender gaze to Lori and her doll. "And yes, my dearest, you are always welcome to bring your doll. I'm sure she is a great comfort to you."

Lori's eyes found his, and an understanding seemed to go between her and this grandfatherly figure.

During all this, Maria had been in her own thoughts, oblivious to the conversation. Was she ready for this? Could she face people? The eyes that could judge, the piteous words that would fall without meaning, and her own hurt guilt still burning inside her.

Until now, a few people had come and visited with her. Holly had become a regular friend, and Sister Bassett came whenever her husband came by to talk about the house plans. However, except for doctors and therapists, she had yet to venture out.

Steve's hand and eyes never left her, and she knew that he was worried about this, too. But she couldn't deny what they had felt, the power and peace. She slightly nodded to Steve as President Hinckle looked up from the kids.

Steve's voice cracked a little. "We'd like that. What time and where should we come?"

Now, as Maria stood in the church foyer, her feelings fluttered from curiosity to fight and flight to peace.

Lois came up to the other side of Jeffrey with Lori and Patrick and smiled reassuringly to Maria.

Steve gently pushed on the small of her back, reminding her of his presence.

She looked around, and a singular painting caught her eye. It was an image of the mortal Christ surrounded by children, and he was smiling. She lingered in the moment of that realization and uniqueness of this image. She had only ever seen Christ in serious expression or pained on the cross. However, she realized that He must have smiled, laughed, and loved as much as he hurt. She resonated with this idea.

Then, a voice disturbed the stillness.

"Maria! I hope it's okay. We saved a place for all of you." It was Sister Basset.

The ever-commanding presence of Sister Basset now had charge of them and guided them from the foyer through another set of doors where pews lined the room. Organ music swelled with unfamiliar tunes, and mixed perfumes from various individuals wafted on the circulating air.

Sister Basset got them situated in a long row between herself and her own family and then proceeded to play gatekeeper to the many curious individuals already there.

How did she know?

Maria breathed a grateful sigh and found the Elders and President Hinckle, each making eye contact as they came in and then moving on.

No one made a big deal of their presence, and no one asked any questions, and all she saw were kind and welcoming smiles.

Steve kept waiting for his habitual skepticism to take hold throughout the meeting. But yet, every speaker, every song, was so honest, he couldn't question the sincerity. All the while, his own belief and understanding grew as well. It all made sense. Nothing felt out of place but instead, seemed to ring true to something he had forgotten long ago, even though he knew that he had never known it in this life.

It went back to what the missionaries and Mr. Hinckle had taught them a few weeks ago. "We lived before this world, forgot it when we came here so that we could learn and grow, and then we will return again to our family and Heavenly Father when we die."

Elder White's face was earnest, and so matter-of-fact, Steve had nearly chuckled. He understood the idea of eternity in theory, but to see the application now as something that could be real before him, it made him wonder what other truths he could find in what he had once thought singularly against faith.

Occasionally, Steve glanced at Maria, anxious for her, and found her eyes locked and intent on every word. He hadn't seen her this peaceful in a long time, and his gratitude echoed as a prayer in his heart.

"Thank you, Father," he silently prayed, and it surprised him how easily the words found their way into his heart and settled there.

In the final hymn, the first words of the verse struck Steve's soul. "The Spirit of God, like a fire is burning...."

His breath caught, an image filled his mind with memories of a menacing glow, and his eyes brimmed with tears.

In the next moment, though, a peaceful warmth spread over him as the words continued, "And Angels are coming to visit the earth."

A distinct presence of individuals seemed to fill the room. Tangible, but invisible. The horrific image was quickly replaced by images of Allan and Sarah smiling, giggling, and running happily into the arms of their grandfather, Michael.

No matter what else, he felt in his heart that this was real and true. Angels truly were visiting the earth, and they were waiting to be reunited one day with loved ones from this earthly existence.

The song finished, a prayer was said, and the family sat still.

Steve tried to process what he had seen and expected his family to feel the same. They all exchanged quick looks, and he somehow knew that they had each experienced something similar.

Holly's voice caught Maria's attention. "I'm so sorry! That was probably not the best song for us to sing today, especially without warning."

Concern filled her face as she wrangled her children to her side, and they impatiently tugged to go wherever they were going next.

Sister Basset joined them and explained, "Yes, they set these songs months in advance, and I didn't even think. Are you okay?"

They had no words, but eventually, Lois said, "It's okay. I think it was a surprise to all of us at first, but then we felt something so beautiful, too."

And, in truth, it really was okay.

Epilogue

CERTAINTY wasn't a word since the fire. Certainty grew into something so much more. Throughout the year, knowledge and understanding of something beyond became a foundation.

Beautiful and hopeful.

Time moved on, but away from the horror, now toward eternity, to become whole once more.

Dressed in white, the family stood around an altar, holding pictures of Michael, Sarah, and Allan. The family was sealed through a special ceremony.

Gazing into the opposing mirrors, they saw themselves go on for eternity, and ministering angels wrapped their arms around them.

There was certainty in this.

There was truth, love, and peace.

There was certainty that found them amid their fiery furnace and brought them home.

The End

ACKNOWLEDGMENTS

*T*HANK YOU to the incredible individuals who have helped me get this story told: Debbie Ihler Rasmussen for guiding and mentoring me to improve my writing like I have never been able to before; Kim Autrey, copywright editor; Kirsten Capuna, cover design facilitator; and Francine Platt, interior designer—for the long hours and willingness to teach and help me through the process. Thank you especially to the entire Author Ready Community. I couldn't have done it without you.

Special thanks to Richard Paul Evans and his mentoring, willingness to teach, guide and inspire me to complete my story.

A very special thanks to the love of my life, Dean Roundy, and his supporting me through everything! Forever is ours I am certain of it!

Printed in the USA
CPSIA information can be obtained
at www.ICGtesting.com
JSHW012147061223
53191JS00002B/2